MORE
CLUE™
MYSTERIES

15 MORE WHODUNITS
TO SOLVE IN MINUTES

BY VICKI CAMERON

RUNNING PRESS
PHILADELPHIA · LONDON

9 8 7 6 5 4
Digit on the right indicates the number of this printing

Library of Congress Control Number 2002096410

ISBN 0-7624-1307-7

Designed by Corinda Cook
Edited by Greg Jones
Typography: Esprit and Copperplate

This book may be ordered by mail from the publisher. Please include $2.50 for postage and
handling.*But try your bookstore first!*

Running Press Book Publishers
125 South Twenty-second Street
Philadelphia, Pennsylvania 19103-4399

Visit us on the web!
www.runningpress.com

CONTENTS

Welcome to Tudor Hall

John Boddy smoothed out the yellowed legal paper on his study desk. So many erudite words: *party of the first part, being of sound mind, without prejudice, estate on trust, responsibilities and entitlements.* They added up to a convoluted and discreet way to say: *don't give my nephew this mansion and my money.*

He gazed around the room. Sir Hugh's study, with its collections of art, atlases, and antique firearms. He'd been master of this house for twelve years, living here for eight, and hadn't the wherewithal to put his personal stamp on it.

All because of this trust fund, his carrot of inheritance dangling from legal phrases. The odd thing about a trust fund was that it meant someone didn't trust you.

Underneath the *hereby bequeaths his estate* section was a separate portion citing *Bequests and Allowances.* Too many names leered up at him from their special paragraphs. What kind of uncle treats his acquaintances better than his own nephew, his only surviving kin? A mean, greedy, self-serving, underhanded uncle who didn't like anyone or anything except money. But that might be putting too fine a point on it.

"Would you care for some tea, Master Boddy?" Mrs. White asked, sensible shoes barging into the study unannounced. She plunked the silver tea tray on the roll-top desk beside his papers.

"I'm twenty-nine, Mrs. White, and will be thirty in a few weeks. I think you ought to start calling me *Mister* Boddy."

"Don't be silly, I was your nanny from when you were twelve. You'll always be Master Boddy to me. Even if I'm just the housekeeper now. What's all this, then?" She pointed at the yellowed papers. "Having a wee look at Sir Hugh's will? Trying to squeeze out an extra tuppence from your allowance?"

"I am verifying facts. Uncle Hugh's trust fund agreement expires on my birthday. The estate, the mansion, the investments, the whole kit and caboodle become mine. All mine."

Mrs. White nodded as she poured the tea. "There's those who will greet that news discontented. Unless you're planning to let them keep their allowances."

"Why should I? What have they done for me? Look at this name. Mrs. Patricia Peacock. I understand she's already spent most of Sir Matthew Peacock's fortune, and he's only been dead nine years."

"Sir Hugh fancied her, that's why he left her an allowance. Might have made an honest woman of her if she hadn't up and married that James Scarlet. You might want to take a close look at her daughter."

"Miss Josephine Scarlet doesn't interest me. She's just another drain on the resources. And an embarrassment, with all those stories in the tabloids about her and rich old men."

"How about me, Mrs. Blanche White? Am I just a drain?"

"No, I rely on you to run the house. So did Uncle Hugh, and he's made it plain in his will."

"So you'll be honoring his wishes and keeping me in pocket?"

"I'll be honoring my own wishes." He stirred his tea and glanced at the plate of shortbread on the silver tray. Her cooking, lamentable on a normal day, could become lethal if she was unhappy. "As I said, I rely on you. I'll review your wages when I rearrange the estate's finances."

"That's better than waiting for you to die to get my inheritance. Keep in mind I'd like to take a trip home to Scotland now and then. Shortbread?"

He took a piece. It melted in his mouth. Mrs. White could bake like an angel, but the rest of her cooking would gag the devil.

"What will you do about that one? Colonel Michael Mustard?" she asked, pointing to another name on the page.

"Colonel Mustard is a pompous old buffoon. You'd think he'd be suitably provided for with his military pension. He shouldn't need Uncle Hugh's handouts any more."

"I wouldn't call it handouts. I'd say it was money to keep his mouth shut. Sir Hugh and the Colonel had quite a time of it when they were both in the Royal Hampshire Regiment."

"I wonder who else is keeping a closed mouth. Professor Peter Plum?" He pointed to the name on the list.

"Like as not he's being paid for services rendered. We've a steady stream of parcels from the Professor when he's in Egypt digging around in the dirt. I hear he's lost his job, too, at the British Museum."

"How about Reverend Mr. John Green? Although I can't picture him with a closed mouth, not when there are souls to save and money to be made."

"Reverend Green indeed. He's no more a licensed clergyman than I'm the Queen of Sheba." Mrs. White spooned sugar into her tea. "Mr. Green masterminded a string of shady deals, I'm sure of it, with Sir Hugh's backing. He'll not settle easily into a new division of the estate."

John Boddy reviewed the list on the yellowed page of the will. None of them would settle easily into a financial rearrangement. He knew what it was like to live with a monthly stipend. He'd been living with one since Uncle Hugh died in 1914. Twelve long years chained to Tudor Hall because he hadn't the means to live elsewhere. Twelve years limping by on a trust fund, waiting for full control of the estate. He was down to counting days until June 18, 1926, when he reached the age of majority, according to Uncle Hugh's twisted idea of what made a man old enough to handle his own money.

"I've an idea," he said, finishing his tea. "I'll throw myself a birthday party. Invite all these people to come and stay for a fortnight. Show them my hospitality. And then show them who controls the purse."

Mrs. White shook her head. "Five guests for a fortnight. Five more rooms to clean, five more beds to make up. Formal dinners and tea served at all hours. Shysters, gold-diggers, strumpets, and buffoons. Who'll make them go home after the party? They'll hang about all summer if no one gives them the boot. And not a shilling more in my pay packet, I'll warrant."

She snatched the tea tray from the desk and marched out of the study. The door slammed shut behind her. The only sounds in the room were the soft creak of the red leather chair and clicking of steel as John Boddy placed the will back in the wall safe.

Back at his desk, he drew out a pile of dove-gray crested letterhead. Invitations. He'd need to send out five letters. *The Pleasure of Your Company is requested at Tudor Hall, Hampshire, on the occasion of the Thirtieth Birthday of Mr. John Boddy.*

If he were a gambling man, he'd wager none of them would have the nerve to stay away.

Trust fund. He didn't trust any of them. They probably didn't trust him. And they wouldn't trust each other.

It would be an interesting two weeks.

THE ROAD
TO GOOD
INTENTIONS

Miss Scarlet pressed her nose to the glass of her bedroom window to get a clearer look at the motor car humming along the driveway toward Tudor Mansion. It was an odd-looking vehicle, shaped rather like a sausage, or a tube of lipstick, only blue. There appeared to be just one seat, occupied by a figure wearing a brown leather helmet, goggles, and a flowing white-fringed scarf.

Drat. She couldn't tell if the driver was a man or a woman, and if a man, if he was handsome or rich. She needed an eligible prospect to liven up the dreary assembly of houseguests. John Boddy ranked high on her list, but he'd spent most of his time so far in his study, working on dusty old papers and crisp dry ledger books. Professor Plum was not too old, but such a studious and vacant fellow. Colonel Mustard was a codger who bored everyone to death with tales of his exploits.

Mother added to the pressure, always carping at her to find a rich young man. Mother didn't oppose her career as an actress, she just opposed the frequent requests for funding while she was between productions. But really, how was a girl to live in the style of actresses without large infusions of cash?

The automobile, motor throbbing, pulled to a stop at the front door, and the occupant climbed out. He was medium height, stocky, wearing an unfortunate green suit under his driving coat. He stood beside the motor car for a few moments like a man who has been cramped in a small space for too long, or like a man who wants everyone to notice his new toy. She wasn't sure which.

She'd better get outdoors or she'd miss all the fun. She finished her makeup and hurried down the stairs. In the main floor passageway, she ran headlong into Professor Plum, trundling to the front hall with his nose buried in a crossword puzzle.

"Oh, I say, so sorry, Miss Scarlet. I didn't see you coming." He pushed his glasses back onto the bridge of his nose and straightened his bow tie. "We're going out to see the motor car. Do you wish to join us? Oh, do join us. Perhaps you know something about automobiles? I'm afraid I'm at a bit of a loss. It looks like some kind of foreign sports car, doesn't it?"

"No, I know nothing about motor cars. I know fashion, though, and that man's suit is a dreadful color." But a man who drives a foreign sports car must have money. A bad suit could be handled adroitly by the right woman, with a little sleight of hand from the closet to the dust bin.

Professor Plum held the front door for her and she delivered an excellent theatrical entrance to the outdoor scene, with her hair tossed back and her skirt fluttering. No one noticed. John Boddy, Colonel Mustard, and Mother were cupping their ears, staring at the motor car. It purred like an oversized lion. The man leaned over and touched something on the dashboard. The engine stopped. The sudden silence was so intense it seemed to suck in all ambient sounds. A few seconds passed before she could hear the rustle of her own skirt in the breeze.

The man took his brown riding coat off and draped it on the motor car seat. His suit was Italian, expensive, a silk and wool blend. If it had been navy, or forest green, it would have been divine, but a Kelly green pinstripe was not a happy choice. It made him look like a parrot. He wrung his hands together like a milliner at the sight of a well-heeled client.

"Mrs. Patricia Peacock," he said, shaking Mother's hand. "How many years has it been since we met in Italy? You were such an elegant young woman then."

"Not many years, I'm sure," Mrs. Peacock said, frowning slightly while her feathered hat danced in the breeze. "This is my daughter, Josephine Scarlet. Josephine, this is the Reverend Mr. John Green."

A Kelly green silk-and-wool-blend sleeve reached toward her. "Miss Scarlet. It is a pleasure to make your acquaintance. You were at boarding school when I last shared a table at a sidewalk café with your mother. Blessed are the plain, for they shall look better in well-tailored clothing. You are twice as beautiful as your photos in the tabloids. The angels would look drab in your presence."

Miss Scarlet shook his pale clammy hand. "Charmed, I'm sure," she said, in the slow drawl she'd learned in Hollywood. He looked older than Mother, with thinning hair and a creased face from too many years in the sun. She did not find him appealing at all, despite the diamond rings and the Italian suit. Unless he was very, very rich she would not encourage him.

"Well, Green, sporting of you to come to the party," Colonel Mustard said. "Haven't seen you since that night we huddled on the roof of a building in Amman, waiting for the sentries to pass. I remember it well. We had slipped up to the roof after dark, which was not entirely on the up-and-up, being as it was past curfew, when suddenly—"

"Never mind that, Colonel, help the Reverend with his bags," Mrs. Peacock said.

"Here you are," Mr. Green said, reaching into the cockpit and pulling out a small pea-green valise and a leather book. He passed the valise to Colonel Mustard, who looked flustered and passed it to Professor Plum. Professor Plum looked surprised and set it on the ground at his feet. Mr. Green leaned over the motor car to shake John Boddy's hand. "Thank you for inviting me to your upcoming birthday party. I look forward to a relaxing couple of weeks here. Nothing like a holiday at a country house, with your feet up, being waited on."

John Boddy said nothing, just ran a finger along the automobile's bonnet.

"That's a lovely motor car, Mr. Green," Miss Scarlet said. "What is it? Why is there only one seat? It seems a fairly large vehicle for only one person."

"This is a Talbot-Darracq Grand Prix racing car. Straight eight 1500 cc supercharged engine. Capable of going very fast. I'd guess more than 200 miles an hour, but I haven't tested it, of course, on the road."

"Interesting sloped radiator grill," Colonel Mustard said. "Gives it a streamlined appearance. Grand Prix, you say? Must be quite a thrill to drive."

"Indeed it is, with the wind rushing by, you can't even hear the engine, you know, the noise is all behind you." Mr. Green folded the leather book to his chest with a supercilious glance at his new housemates. "In a motor like this, you can outrun the police without trying."

"I've seen this motor car before, in Italy." Mrs. Peacock said. "I remember because it's French blue. I find it most attractive. A dear friend showed it to me in the factory. It was under construction then, all hush-hush and men tinkering under the bonnet. I thought they were going to run it in this year's Grand Prix."

"Vehicles come and go," Mr. Green said. "Sometimes they think they have a winner and something better comes along."

"Can I drive it?" Miss Scarlet asked. "Down to the village and back?" Anything to liven up the tedium of hanging about in Tudor Mansion waiting for a silly birthday party in a fortnight's time.

"One needs a certain spectrum of knowledge to drive a motor car," Mrs. Peacock said. "Do you have it, Josephine?"

Miss Scarlet was spared the necessity of answering by Mrs. White marching out of the front door with arms folded across her apron.

"There's some Italian fellow on the phone. Emilio Materassi, I think he said. Shouting about wanting to talk to Reverend Black. I told him Sir Hugh Black was not a reverend, and anyway he's been dead these twelve years. Then there's Master Boddy, who is sometimes called Doctor Black by the locals, but he's not a reverend either. He got all emotional, so I hung up. I suppose you'll all want tea now that Mr. Green has arrived."

"And my bag taken to my room, if you don't mind, Mrs. White," Mr. Green said, pointing at the valise at Professor Plum's feet. "Mr. Boddy, have you a spare spot in your garage? I don't like to leave my motor car exposed to the weather. Open cockpit, as you can see."

The four men strolled toward the garage, Mr. Green pontificating about carburetors and spark plugs.

Mrs. White picked up the valise. "There's that telephone ringing. I hope it's not that Materassi fellow again. He's called twice already. Seems sure Sir Hugh Black is a man of the cloth." She stalked into the house.

Mrs. Peacock and Miss Scarlet were left standing beside the motor car.

"I know Emilio Materassi," Mrs. Peacock said, nudging a tire with a delft blue pump. "He's not the type to make errors where people's names are concerned. He's a wealthy man, quite charming when he wants to be. Bit of a race car enthusiast. He'd be interested in this one, I'm sure. If he met you, he'd paint one of his motor cars red."

Miss Scarlet mulled that over throughout the dreary evening listening to Colonel Mustard relate one of his terminally boring stories. Imagine a red race car named *Josephine* winning the Grand Prix. She could have her picture taken leaning on the bonnet. She'd get acting jobs all over the country. Maybe this Emilio person would take a fancy to her, and her days of near-poverty would be over. It was too tedious, being poor, and having to make do with last month's fashions.

Professor Plum fell asleep on his crossword, his glasses slipped sideways on his nose. Mr. Green pretended to be reading his leather book, but he did little more than gaze vacantly and turn the pages occasionally with his stubby pointed fingers. John Boddy and Colonel Mustard engaged in a serious game of cribbage. The telephone rang repeatedly, and Miss Scarlet kept hearing Mrs. White's sensible shoes on the hardwood, running down the passageway from the kitchen to the library to answer it. If she were the lady of the house, she'd have telephones installed in all the rooms, not just the study and the library. But then, Mrs. White was not the lady of the house, just the housekeeper.

In the morning, lying in her vermilion four poster bed looking at the bright blue sky, Miss Scarlet had an idea. While they were all eating breakfast, tucking back toast and tea, she'd take that motor car for a drive. How hard could it be, driving a motor car? She'd sat beside young men while they drove. They simply pushed forward on the stick and stamped on the accelerator. They seemed to play with the stick thingy frequently, but that was obviously manly posturing to make themselves look important. The motor cars seemed to carry on regardless.

She slipped out of bed and dressed in a clingy poppy red chiffon outfit and matching Italian shoes. Downstairs smelled of burned toast. In the front hall she found Mr. Green's leather helmet, goggles, and white scarf.

She put them on. An open cockpit was an invitation to dirt in the hair and eyes, and the scarf looked snazzy. The telephone was ringing again. She could hear it in the study.

She tiptoed out the front door and around the drive to the garage. It was a tidy garage, with two motor cars lined up neatly, three rakes, a shovel, and a ladder against one wall. She found the race car draped in dust cloths like a house's furniture when the family was going away to the Continent for the summer. She pulled the drapery away, opened the garage doors, and eased into the narrow leather seat. There was precious little room to spare in the cockpit. She couldn't see where she would place a picnic basket or a parcel from the shops. Well, it didn't matter. She wasn't going on a picnic and she had no money to spend in the shops. Not until Mother caved in to her requests.

Nevertheless, today's goal was a simple joy ride. Take the motor car on a tour of the village and the countryside, and be back in time for coffee at elevenses.

She studied the stick. It had lots of numbers and lines on it, and the letter 'R'. Reverse, that's what that meant, she was sure. Used for backing up. She'd start with that one, to get out of the garage.

An array of dials covered the dashboard. Lots of numbers and needles, and some of them had red wedges painted behind them. Tucked into a narrow pocket on the door were a couple of sheets of paper. One had a checklist, a column of little boxes with words beside each. It was all in Italian, so she couldn't read a word, but it looked like the motor car had passed some kind of test. The other sheet was a map of what looked like a race track, with checkered flags marking a line across it. Under the map was an official looking form, with words written on lines, and a signature at the bottom. All in Italian, again, so she couldn't understand it, or read the messy signature.

She noticed a line of foot pedals. These must be like little footstools, handy places to rest the feet. She placed her feet on two of them. They were loose. She pushed. The motor car rolled forward.

She pulled her feet back. The motor car stopped. How could the motor car move if the motor wasn't running?

The others would be finishing breakfast by now, wandering from the back of the house to the front, carrying cups of tea and aimlessly searching for something to do until coffee time. She ought to get started on her joy ride. She'd been on several joy rides at Miss Puce's School for Girls, but always in the back seat, often holding a bundle of something nicked from the kitchen or from Miss Puce's classroom. There was no back seat in this motor car.

She turned the ignition key. The engine sputtered. This was vexing. Young men had no trouble starting motor cars. She put her feet on the pedals and pushed. The motor car rolled forward again. She turned the key. The engine started with a roar. Good gracious, it was noisy. She'd have to get out of the garage quickly before Mr. Green heard the rumbling and rushed out to stop her. She pushed the stick into the 'R' position and wondered what to do with her feet. She noticed another foot pedal, a bigger one, so she dropped her right foot onto it and pushed. The engine roared. That must be the accelerator. It ought to make the motor car go fast, but pressing it made the motor car too noisy and echoing in the garage. She moved her left foot off the small pedal. The motor car shot back out of the garage, across the driveway, onto the lawn, and stopped abruptly when it rammed into an oak tree. The goggles did an admirable job of protecting her eye makeup from the steering wheel.

Good. She was out of the garage. She had a clear run at the driveway if she just turned the steering wheel. She pushed the stick forward to number '1', played with the combinations of foot pedals again, and the motor car lurched forward. She pressed harder on the accelerator. The engine snarled and the motor car took off like a pea off the end of a flicked spoon.

She yanked at the steering wheel when the motor car was back on the driveway, and the vehicle spun around with a plume of gravel. Wonderful. She was headed in the right direction. This driving business was easy. Imagine Mother quibbling about necessary knowledge. She knew everything she needed to know already. She pressed her right foot harder on the pedal and the motor car zoomed forward down the driveway.

Hurray! She was driving! She pressed harder and harder on the accelerator. The motor car screamed and snarled, but it didn't seem to go much faster. For a race car, it moved uncommonly slowly. She ought to be halfway to the village by now, instead of puttering down the driveway. Mr. Green had said it could outrun the police. It could barely outrun a squirrel.

The engine reverberated. Mr. Green said the noise was left behind you at high speed, but it seemed to be all around her, thundering in her ears even through the protective leather helmet. She'd just have to go faster. She pushed harder on the pedal. One of the needles sprang up into the red zone on the dial. The other needle inched up. If it recorded the speed, she wanted to put it to the highest number.

When she glanced up again, she was hurtling toward the mansion gates, and they were closed.

She twisted the steering wheel sharply and the motor car spun around in a circle. She threw her hands up to cover her face. The motor car straightened and sped onward, back up the driveway toward the mansion. This was not what she wanted. She'd have to get the gates open somehow. They were iron, so it didn't seem like a good idea to ram them. She might scratch the paint on the motor car.

Gripping the steering wheel, she pressed harder and harder on the pedal. The motor car shuddered and howled.

Oh, no. The noise had roused the house.

The front door of Tudor Mansion spilled people onto the steps. Mr. Green waved both hands at her. Colonel Mustard slashed the air with his riding crop, making some kind of repetitive gesture. Mother clutched her throat and Mrs. White brandished a rolling pin. Professor Plum had both hands to his face. If she got close enough, she'd be able to see the whites of his eyes behind his glasses. Yes, now she could see them. He looked terrified.

They all seemed to be shouting something at her, but she couldn't hear over the thunderous vroom of the engine.

Oops, she ought to turn the steering wheel or she'd be driving up the steps and into the front hall. She yanked hard to the right. The motor car spun out again, showering the steps with gravel.

Now she was headed across the lawn. Not the joy ride she had in mind. Bracing herself with her right foot against the accelerator, she turned and waved at the assemblage on the steps, who now seemed to be chasing her.

"Open the gates!" she shouted at them, waving her hands in the direction of the iron gates. "Open the gates, please!"

Mother's hands flew to shield her eyes. Mrs. White turned away with both arms covering her head. What now? Didn't they hear her?

She swiveled back in the seat and looked ahead. The motor car was rocketing straight for the ornamental pond. It was also making a strange clunking screaming noise, followed by a huge bang and a hiss of steam.

She ought to stop. Really, she ought to. How do drivers make motor cars stop?

The motor car plunged shrieking into the water. Steam billowed around her, and she could feel herself sinking.

Oh, dear. This wasn't a good ending for a joy ride. Her new frock was going to get wet, unless someone carried her out of the cockpit to safety. Yes, that would be a good idea. She stood up on the seat and held her arms out. They were running toward her, all of them, still shouting, but her ears were ringing from the engine noises.

Her feet were wet. Water poured in over the sides of the cockpit. The motor car was sinking into the brackish water. Even the lily pads were recoiling in disgust.

The helpful guests had stopped on the edge of the pond. No one seemed ready and willing to wade in to save her. She scrambled out onto the tubular body of the motor car. She could stand there until they roused themselves. "Help," she shouted. "Will someone come and get me?"

She took a couple of steps forward, and her toe caught on a rumpled piece of metal and tree bark. Unbalanced, she fell.

In the next instant she was submerged under brown scummy water full of hissing bubbles. She struggled for the surface.

When she regained her equilibrium, she was standing armpit deep in murky water. Her outfit was surely ruined, and her hair. Still no one ventured to rescue her. There was nothing for it but to stride forward with courage and dignity. It was a struggle, with the mud sucking at her feet.

On the shore, she yanked off the helmet and goggles and glared at them. "Why didn't someone try to save me? Look, one of my shoes is missing and my clothing is destroyed. And this scarf will never be white again."

"My motor car, my motor car!" Mr. Green tore at the remaining tufts of his hair. "What have you done to my motor car? Didn't you hear us screaming at you to change gears? You've stripped the gears, blown a piston and drowned the entire automobile!"

"And crumpled the back end," Colonel Mustard offered.

"It might never run again!" Mr. Green thrashed at the air with pudgy fists. "How dare you!"

"It wasn't very fast anyway," she said. "I don't see why it was called a race car. And it was so noisy."

"Honestly, Josephine, the liberties you take with other people's valuables." Mrs. Peacock shook her head. "You had no right to steal this motor car. You don't know how to drive, that's clear."

"I've got to get my motor car out of that water, immediately. I'll get a rope." Mr. Green sprinted toward the house.

Colonel Mustard started gesturing with his riding crop again. "Change gears, Miss Scarlet. Did you not see me showing you how to change gears? Like this." He waved the riding crop through the pattern again. "Depress the clutch and change gears. Did you not notice the tachometer running too high?"

"What's a tachometer?"

"A dial that shows you how many revolutions per minute the motor is turning at."

"Does it have a sweet little red wedge on it? That one had the needle in the red section. It looked smart there, black needle on red background. Why isn't the rest of the dial red?"

Colonel Mustard shook his head like a man defeated. "They shall never believe this story down at the Officer's Club."

"I say, the motor car's completely disappeared," Professor Plum said staring at the water. "I don't suppose that will be good for the engine."

"I don't think the engine was in good shape when she hit the water, Plum," Colonel Mustard said. "Like as not she's blown a piston. Green will have to take the train back to London after the holiday."

"Doesn't anyone notice that my frock is ruined? I'll have to go shopping. Mother?"

"Shopping? I suppose you think I ought to buy you a new frock. After an escapade like this, I think not. Did you learn nothing at Miss Puce's school?"

Miss Scarlet thought about how she had learned to fill balloons with water and drop them from the casement windows. "Apparently I didn't learn the right things. The useful things." Although the balloon trick had been most useful in staging a diversion while some of the older girls sneaked out for the evening.

"You'll be wanting a bath, and a nice cup of tea after that dunking," Mrs. White said. "I'll get to it." She turned and walked back across the rutted lawn to the mansion.

Mr. Green came back driving the other motor car, and got out with a rope in one hand. "I'll tie this on the back bumper of this vehicle, and use it to drag mine out. Colonel, could you tie this to the submerged motor car?"

Colonel Mustard coughed. "I'm an officer, dear boy. Officers issue the orders. Plum, take this end of the rope. Green, take the other end. Plum, wade into the water. I'll direct you. Green, do you know how to tie a sheepshank knot?"

Professor Plum stared down at his purple tweeds. "I've only the one pair of pants."

"Mrs. White will spruce them up overnight for you," Colonel Mustard said. "Or the ladies will excuse us and you can take off most of your kit. Hop to it. Orders are orders."

Mrs. Peacock frowned. "I think a great deal of mud is going to come of this. Come along, Josephine, and we'll see about cleaning you up."

Miss Scarlet followed Mother back to the mansion and found Mrs. White had drawn a hot bubble bath. In half an hour, she was fresh as a kitten and twice as cute, according to the mirror.

Downstairs she found consternation in the halls. A muddy track led from the front hall to the study. Professor Plum's face was streaked with pond scum and a lily pad lay on his hair. He looked like a man wearing dry clothes and wet underwear. Mr. Green's silk and wool blend Kelly green pinstriped pants were wet to the knees. Colonel Mustard was blocking the study door with his riding crop. The others crowded around, trying to peek past him.

"Steady on, keep clear," he said. "No one is allowed in until the authorities have arrived."

"What's going on?" Miss Scarlet asked.

"Boddy has been dispatched, with a rope by the looks of it. It's not a pretty sight. Not suitable for the eyes and sensibilities of a young lady. Keep clear, I say."

"He was on the telephone with that Materassi," Mrs. White said. "I heard him telling the man he understood, and would fix it. I believe his exact words were 'make the scoundrel pay'."

"When was this?" Mrs. Peacock asked.

"After breakfast, when you'd all gone off with your final cups of tea, and leaving the empties in every room for me to collect. He was still talking to him when I closed the door and carried on to the library."

"Where was everyone, then?" Colonel Mustard asked. "Account for yourselves, please. I went to the conservatory for a little air."

"I went to the library to find the day's newspaper," Professor Plum said. "Mrs. White took my cup, although I wasn't quite finished."

"I came to the hall to see if the post had arrived," Mr. Green said.

"I went to the lounge, as I always do," Mrs. Peacock said.

"I was in the kitchen washing up," Mrs. White said. "After I had collected all the cups."

All eyes turned to Miss Scarlet.

"You weren't at breakfast," Colonel Mustard said. "You were in the study killing Boddy."

Miss Scarlet stepped to the front door and opened it. Outside, the race car sat in the driveway, tethered to the larger motor car and sluicing water from every joint. She turned back to the group huddled around the study door.

"I accuse you of killing John Boddy in the study with the rope," she said.

THE ROAD TO GOOD INTENSIONS

SOLUTION:

Mrs. Peacock sighed. "Don't be so theatrical, Josephine, just because you are an actress."

"I think we all know where I was. I was sneaking out to drive the race car. I tiptoed through this hall, and I didn't see you here." She pointed at Mr. Green. "If you'd been here in the ten minutes after I'd passed though, you'd have heard me starting the motor car and would have come out to investigate."

"More's the pity he didn't," Mrs. Peacock said. "We would have been spared that fiasco on the lawn."

"Besides, there was no rope in the garage. It was remarkably empty of tools," Miss Scarlet added. "But you knew exactly where to find a rope to tow your race car out of the pond. You had already used it to kill John."

"Why would I kill Mr. Boddy?" Mr. Green asked, pulling himself up tall and haughty even though his pant legs and wing tip shoes were clotted with swampy water and mud.

"Because of that motor car, I guess. That Materassi person was looking for Reverend Black. You gave him a false name when you stole his motor car. What were you doing, taking it out for a blessing?"

Colonel Mustard nodded. "Easy enough to find an English gentleman named Black by calling the better clubs and inquiring."

"I didn't think Emilio Materassi would part with that motor car after the money he poured into it," Mrs. Peacock said. "He's very keen on winning the Grand Prix."

"With another motor car, perhaps," Mr. Green protested. "That one wasn't up to snuff."

"But Emilio's terribly anxious to win," Mrs. Peacock continued. "I think he would fall victim to a preacher offering to guarantee a successful race by driving around the block for a Higher Power."

"I found some papers in the motor car," Miss Scarlet said. "They were in Italian, so I couldn't read them, but one seemed to be a mechanic's test results, and everything was good. The other looked like an entry form for the race, signed."

Colonel Mustard poked Mr. Green in the chest with his riding crop. "We shall see about those papers, Green. I rather think Mrs. Peacock could read a bit of Italian."

"I'd know Emilio's signature, certainly." Mrs. Peacock stalked toward the front door. "We'll have this straightened out in a few minutes, if the ink hasn't all run in the water. Emilio will be livid if you've ruined his race car."

Mrs. Peacock, Mrs. White, and Professor Plum hurried out the front door to the dripping automobile.

Miss Scarlet frowned at Mr. Green. "I hope you realize what you've done. I've lost a shoe in that pond. It was Italian, too."

THE SCONE
OF STONE

A lorry cruised up the long lane of Tudor Hall in the moonlight and stopped under a grove of trees, hidden from the inquisitive windows of the mansion. Two laborers slumped out and went about their business at the rear of the vehicle.

Two gentlemen stood under the trees watching.

"Where'd'ya want it, guv'nor?" one of the laborers asked.

The taller gentleman pointed to a flat spot beside a yew tree.

The laborers struggled with their load and deposited it in the designated location. Money changed hands. The laborers climbed in the lorry and drove away.

The two gentlemen watched the truck disappear out the mansion gates before either spoke.

"It's not what I expected," the taller man said, running his fingers along the glossy surface of the low object.

"You expected that fake clinker people have been mooning over for the last 700 years," the other man said. "This is the real thing. As old as time. I did a lot of digging to find it. Trust me, this is the original. Worth a fortune. You'll thank me for it in the morning."

Money changed hands.

Colonel Michael Mustard strode into the lounge for elevenses. Mrs. Peacock was already there, draped across the chintz chesterfield, preening in a silly blue feathered hat. If she didn't shift over he'd be obliged to stand for morning coffee. He hated juggling cup, saucer, and shortbread. He hoped it would be shortbread today, made from a Scottish recipe handed down in Mrs. White's family for generations.

Mr. Green had his nose buried in a leather-bound book, and judging by his drooping eyes the plot must have been less than riveting. He had a bag of sweets beside him on his green leather chair. Professor Plum huddled in the other leather chair, his glasses askew, his pen scratching at the crossword puzzle in the newspaper. Miss Scarlet had not yet made an appearance, as it was not yet noon. Good. He couldn't abide her vacuous prattle. It would be a long summer if she stayed on after John Boddy's pivotal birthday party. He intended to stay on, regardless. Not that he was pinching pennies, but free lodging ought not to be relinquished just because the party was over.

"Oh, there you are, Colonel," Mrs. Peacock said. "Would you care to join me?" She made a slight movement of her slender ankles, as if to send them to the floor where they belonged, with the effort of a cat lying in the sun.

"Not at the moment, Mrs. Peacock. I'll take a tour around the room, keep myself limber. When the coffee arrives, I shall be delighted to share the chesterfield."

There, let her take her time but make it clear her feet must vacate the seat. He strolled toward the windows and peered past the green velvet drapes out over the lawn. "Looks like a new lawn ornament out there beside the yew tree. I dare say Boddy is expecting an overflow crowd at his party. It appears to be a seat of some kind."

"I say, what?" Professor Plum asked, looking up from his puzzle. "A party seat? Is someone running for office?"

"I don't think we should go around sitting on the lawn ornaments," Mr. Green said, yawning. "You wouldn't sit on a tombstone. Why sit on the bric-a-brac?"

"Because it's there, I suppose," Mrs. Peacock said. "If one is tired and a suitable piece of sculpture presents itself, one sits."

"No one should ever sit on a piece of sculpture, in case of damage," Professor Plum said. "Even stone artifacts must be treated with extreme care."

"What, in case they break? It's awfully difficult to break a stone." Mrs. Peacock glanced at her hand. "Not like fingernails. They break easily."

Colonel Mustard stifled a shudder. If he didn't speak up quickly and change the subject, Mrs. Peacock would start going on about style and grooming. He turned away from the windows and cast about for some topic of conversation. Ah-ha. Green's paper bag. "Been to the shops this morning, Green?" he asked.

"I have indeed." Mr. Green dipped a pudgy hand into the bag and popped a handful of sweets in his mouth. "Enjoyed a little stroll to the village and picked out a few bob's worth of the finest at the village sweet shop. Blessed are the hungry, for they shall be filled with sugar. Bought myself a new pen, too. Mine seem to have a habit of disappearing." He frowned in Professor Plum's direction while licking his fingers.

Professor Plum dropped the pen he was using and let it roll between the cushion and the chair arm. He patted his pockets and came up with a pencil.

"That looks like gold to me, Mr. Green," Mrs. Peacock said. "I imagine you paid handsomely for it. You ought to keep it in your inner pocket."

The door burst open and Mrs. White marched in with a full silver tray. She dropped it on the circular inlaid cherry table, and the cups rattled. "There's your elevenses, then. Coffee and scones. I'll be off to the kitchen to find that mouse and give him what for." She flounced out the door, slamming it behind her.

"I say, she is in a state," Professor Plum said. "It's not like our Mrs. White to risk breaking the cups. Oh, these scones are still hot. Right from the oven."

Colonel Mustard found his route to the scones blocked by Green's greedy hand. He withdrew and retrenched. Mrs. Peacock picked up the coffee pot. He swooped in neatly with his cup and allowed her to pour. Good strong coffee it was, too. The crowd of hands around the scone plate thinned. He selected two scones and settled onto the chesterfield while Mrs. Peacock was busy sitting upright pouring the coffee.

"Who do you think invented scones," Professor Plum asked. "Do you think it was something like the Earl of Sandwich, who invented sandwiches because he didn't want to stop playing cards long enough to eat with a knife and fork?"

"You mean, did the Bishop of Scone Palace want a little something to tide him over until dinner?" Mrs. Peacock asked. "Or did he find shortbread too sweet?"

"What in blazes?" Mr. Green stared at his scone. Crumbs jiggled on the edge of his lips.

"What is it this time?" Mrs. Peacock asked. "Flies in place of currants? Rancid butter?"

"No, it's, I don't know, it's—" He licked his lips and tried again.

"Quite so," Professor Plum said through a mouthful of scone. "Grit?"

Colonel Mustard took a tentative bite of his scone. His teeth crunched.

The scone maintained its integrity. He tried again. The scone snapped in two and the smaller chunk lodged in his cheek. He tried chewing and the scone resisted. "Goodness," he said.

"Pebbles," Mrs. Peacock sputtered. "Sand."

"Rock," Mr. Green said.

"Stone." Colonel Mustard swilled coffee and swallowed. "Scones of stone. What does that woman do in the kitchen?"

Mrs. Peacock dabbed her lips. "Those are quite atrocious. Dry as dust. Hard as rock."

"A bad recipe?" Professor Plum suggested. "Maybe they'll soften up if dunked in the coffee."

"I think she's forgotten an ingredient," Mrs. Peacock said, picking at a scone with a cautious fingernail. "Something must have upset her while she was measuring. I suspect she forgot the sugar. Or the baking powder."

"She mentioned a mouse." Professor Plum took out his magnifying glass and examined the black bits in his scone. "I believe these are actually currants."

Colonel Mustard stared at the one-and-a-half scones resting in his saucer. They were inedible. He could leave the half on his saucer, but he'd have to dispose of the untouched one somehow. He couldn't eat it, and he couldn't slide it back onto the serving plate. He slipped it into the pocket of his uniform.

The door flew open. Miss Scarlet pirouetted into the room, a study in dishevelment. Her brown hair fluttered like a flock of angry sparrows. She swept the train of her pink satin dressing gown around her feet with high drama. "Something dreadful has happened," she announced. "I must have coffee."

"Yes, we know," Mrs. Peacock said. "Mrs. White has erred in baking. You are too late to warn us not to eat the scones."

Miss Scarlet pounced on the coffee and downed a full cup before speaking again. "No, much worse. John Boddy is dead. I just tripped over him in the conservatory. There's a knife sticking out of his back."

Scones dropped to the floor from every hand. Colonel Mustard dropped his half, and regretted having spirited the other into his pocket. He'd have to go outside later and visit some shrubbery to discard it. Let the squirrels choke on it.

"Order, order, we must have order," he said, tapping his riding crop on the Oriental rug. "I shall take charge of the situation. You will all remain here while I accompany Miss Scarlet to the scene of the crime."

He strode to the door and opened it. Miss Scarlet swept out before him like a cabaret singer leaving the floor after a standing ovation. Behind him he heard the patter and stomp of several other feet. Dash it all, they were following him. That destroyed his idea of jettisoning his scone into the pot of an aspidistra while he contained the crime scene.

He carried on to the conservatory, where the sun glittered on the knife which did indeed protrude from Boddy's back, just as Miss Scarlet had claimed. He knelt down beside the body and felt for a pulse. He felt nothing, but heard the crunching of many feet collecting around him. He glanced around. The floor was sprinkled with a white dust of some sort, and now the dust bore the footprints of every person in the house.

"Do you mind?" He waved them back with his riding crop. "Please step away from the deceased."

Feet shuffled back, and the white dust smudged. They'd be tracking it all down the passageway. Mrs. White would not be amused.

"I say, is he dead?" Professor Plum asked. "That is a bit of a blow."

"Yes, he is, sad to say. I shall alert the authorities. I must have this area clear. Please return to the lounge."

"What, and miss all the fun?" Miss Scarlet asked. "What are you looking for in that aspidistra pot, Colonel?"

"Clues, Miss Scarlet. And I don't see any." He pushed the scone back into his pocket.

"What about this?" Mrs. Peacock said, picking up a little notebook from the floor near Boddy's outstretched arm. "It looks like a personal journal, in Mr. Boddy's handwriting. Let's see what he has to say in his last entry."

Mr. Green seized it from her hand. "My dear lady, that contains the private ruminations of the deceased. It would be sacrilege to read it. Blessed are the discreet, for they shall inherit secrets."

"Maybe so," Miss Scarlet said, snatching it from him, "but it will be fun reading. See, here's an entry from yesterday. *Shipment arriving tonight. Couldn't be more pleased. Imagine I'll have to pay exorbitant fee for services. But the glory, owning Destiny.*"

"Do tell," Mrs. Peacock said. "I wonder if Destiny is a race horse." She peered over Miss Scarlet's shoulder. "Oh, look, he wrote something else after that. *Destiny on lawn. Not what I expected. Guaranteed to be the genuine article. Paid too much if it isn't. A bargain if it is. Can't be sure in the dark. Wait until I tell M—* Well, it can't be a horse, then. There is no mistaking a real horse from an imposter."

"Unless it's the difference between a pedigreed animal and a hack," Professor Plum offered. "You might not be able to tell the difference in the dark."

"Poppycock, all of it," Mr. Green said. "Nothing but idle contemplations from a man with too much time on his hands. None of it means anything." He rocked back on his heels, and his glossy wingtip shoes squeaked.

"Give me that book," Colonel Mustard demanded, holding out his hand. "I shall have to hand it to the authorities as evidence."

"Not before I find out what John had to say about me." Miss Scarlet flipped back through pages, scanning the neat script for her name.

Colonel Mustard lifted the journal from her hands and tucked it into his uniform breast pocket. "There'll be no more of that. Off with you, all of you. To the lounge. Wait for further instructions."

He shooed them out the door and closed it firmly. First, the scone in his pocket. It would be imprudent to jettison it at the scene of the crime. A trip outside at his earliest convenience was the solution to that problem.

Second, the body. Sprawled on the floor near the fountain. Bits of grass stuck to the shoes. He searched around for other clues and found a fountain pen under the chaise longue and a half cup of tea on the table. Boddy might have been sitting in that chair writing in his journal, enjoying his tea, and then been stabbed. However, he was not stabbed in the back while sitting in the chair, so he must have gotten up and walked toward the fountain, carrying both pen and journal. Picking up the pen and taking the journal from his pocket, Colonel Mustard recreated that scenario. He sat in the chair, got up, and walked toward the fountain.

What happened next? Someone came up behind Boddy and stabbed him. Boddy dropped the pen and journal, and the pen rolled under the chair.

Colonel Mustard walked as far as Boddy's feet and threw his hands up as if he had been stabbed. The pen landed in the vicinity of the chaise longue, and the journal dropped closer to Boddy's hand.

That was a reasonable explanation, verified by reenactment. It didn't explain the white dust on the floor, but he was a military man, not a police officer. They'd have to figure that out for themselves. He'd lock the door of the conservatory, call the authorities, and get out to the garden before they arrived and looked in his pockets.

A few minutes later he strolled toward the rose bushes with one hand braced in his pocket for the quick toss. He heard voices calling around the corner of the mansion. Why could the others not follow instructions? He'd specifically told them to wait in the lounge. Now they were lolly-gagging around the lawn, shouting something as if they were calling the dog to go for a walk. They would be upon him at any moment. Speed was of the essence. He tossed. The scone tumbled down through the rose leaves and lodged on a thorn. He jabbed at it with his riding crop until it slid down closer to the ground and the foliage hid it from view.

"Whatever are you doing, Colonel?" Mrs. Peacock asked. "Smelling the roses?"

"We could use some help here, looking for Destiny," Professor Plum said. "Do you think horses come when they're called? Destiny, here boy, here girl!"

"If Destiny's a dog, it's a badly behaved one. I've been calling for ages. I am quite worn out." Miss Scarlet slumped onto the stone seat beside the yew tree and arranged her dressing gown decoratively around her feet. "I suppose I should take my bath before the police get here and cordon off the tub."

Colonel Mustard turned his back on the rose bush in question to shield it from view. "What ho, that's the new stone seat I noticed through the window this morning. It's quite attractive."

"White marble," Professor Plum said. "If I get a closer look I'll be able to tell you if it's Italian or Greek. There are differences, you know, as any archeologist can deduce."

"I'm sure it's very old, as stones go," Mr. Green said, wiping his damp hands on his leaf green jacket. "Let there be dirt, and there was dirt."

"It's more of a footstool than a chair." Miss Scarlet wiggled on the seat to make it more comfortable. "It ought to be higher, and wider. Maybe we can get someone to put some supports under it to raise it." She ran her fingers along the surface. "It's got some pretty carving on it, though. Symbols. Can you decipher them, Professor?"

"I might, but you'd have to get up."

"But I don't want to. I'm quite enjoying the rest."

"Anyone care for more?" Mrs. White marched toward them across the lawn carrying a tray of scones.

Colonel Mustard turned around and shuddered. Was Mrs. White offering more of the wretched stone scones?

Mrs. White screamed and dropped the plate. The scones bounced away on the grass. "Get up! Get off that seat! How dare you!" She yanked Miss Scarlet off the stone bench by her sleeves. "Begging your pardon, Miss."

"Well, I never," Miss Scarlet said, wrapping her dressing gown more tightly. "What do you mean by this? I was just sitting on the new bench."

"I'm sorry, but you can't. Nobody sits on the Stone of Destiny. Nobody but the true kings of Scotland."

"The Stone of Destiny? You mean the Stone of Scone?" Mrs. Peacock asked, her feathered hat fluttering.

"I say, let's have a look," Professor Plum said. He knelt down beside the stone and ran his fingers over the markings. "Celtic cross, Celtic knots, Gaelic. Oh, I say, this is interesting." He pulled out a magnifying glass and studied the marks.

"Is this the Stone of Destiny?" Mrs. Peacock asked. "Is this the Destiny we've been seeking? And all the time we've been calling a horse."

"Hmm, what?" Professor Plum said, looking distracted. "The Stone of Destiny is in Westminster, as part of the royal coronation throne. This isn't that stone. That stone is yellow sandstone. This one is white marble. That one has a Latin cross inscribed on it. This one has many other markings."

"That one at Westminster is the lid of a cesspool," Mrs. White declared. "This one has been at Scone Palace since 1296. You don't think the Scots were fool enough to give King Edward I the real stone, do you, when they had six weeks warning that he was coming to take it away? They used the time to provide another. They fobbed him off with a fake." Mrs. White waved a fist in the air. "The Scots own the true Stone of Destiny. It's been at Scone these last 700 years, waiting the restoration of the true kings of Scotland. And back it will go, just as soon as I contact the League of Scottish Poets and Patriots."

Mrs. Peacock clucked her tongue. "This isn't the Stone of Scone. I've been to Scone to visit the present Earl, and he showed me the Stone. It's yellow limestone. Just like the one in Westminster. Not a bit like this one."

Colonel Mustard tapped his riding crop against the stone. "Order, order I say. I accuse you of stabbing Boddy with a knife in the conservatory."

THE SCONE
OF STONE

SOLUTION:

Miss Scarlet stamped her slippered foot. "I did not. Just because John didn't write about me in his journal is no reason to suspect me."

"Allow me to reconstruct the scene," Colonel Mustard said. "This stone was not here yesterday, so it must have arrived overnight. Boddy's shoes have bits of dried grass stuck to them, indicating he had been out walking on the dewy grass in the early morning. Afterwards, he sat in the conservatory to write in his journal. That was right after breakfast as he had a half cup of tea, not coffee. Someone came in and he gloated about his new acquisition. Bragged to his visitor that he was now the owner of the one true Stone of Scone. That person was so enraged, she dropped her cup of sugar and stabbed him with a kitchen knife."

Mrs. White folded her arms across her apron.

"And so the scones were ruined, because when she returned to the kitchen, she forgot to replace the sugar." Mrs. Peacock nodded. "I knew it was the sugar."

Mrs. White glared at them. "He told me all about it. Told me he had bought the true Stone of Scone for his garden, and the Scottish Poets and Patriots could complain all they liked, he wasn't going to give it up. I was furious. All these years Scotland has been protecting the true Stone of

Destiny, and an idle rich youngster thinks he can do them out of it. The knife just happened to be right handy in my hand."

Colonel Mustard nodded. "Plum says this doesn't look like the Stone of Scone from Westminster. Mrs. Peacock says it is not the stone she saw at Scone. Someone was paid for finding this stone. Someone who had enough money today to buy a gold pen. That person knows the provenance of this stone."

Eyes swiveled to Mr. Green.

"Who's to say if either the stone at Westminster or the stone at Scone is the real one?" Mr. Green wrung his pudgy hands. "There have been many tales and rumors. Legend has it that the original stone was used by the Irish kings and it was white marble. It's been hidden at Tara all these years. St. Patrick himself blessed it and the Irish kings were crowned on it. This looks like the real thing to me."

"Unless you translate the Gaelic," Professor Plum said, putting away his magnifying glass. "These markings say 'Jameson Fine Irish Whiskey Since 1780.' I dare say the distillery's got a blank spot on its front lawn today."

RECIPE
FOR
DISASTER

"Psst. Mrs. Peacock. Come and look at this."

Mr. Green beckoned to her from the passageway. She was the only one he could think of who could see a reason behind the mess in the library, so soon after lunch.

Mrs. Peacock straightened her feathered hat and followed him. He led her to the library door and stood with his arm out, presenting the scene for her approval.

"What do you think, Mrs. Peacock?"

"I see many books open and spread out all over the reading table. Someone must be looking for something interesting to read. Someone who expects someone else to pick up after her. My daughter, Josephine."

"No, you're missing the point. Look at them." He ushered her closer. "*Mrs. Lincoln's Boston Cook Book. The Woman Suffrage Cook Book.*"

"*The Enterprising Housekeeper, The Boston Cooking-School Cook Book, The Frugal Housewife.* Ah. I see what you mean. They're all recipe books."

"Yes. Exactly. Now do you see the problem?"

Mrs. Peacock paled. "Oh, dear, yes. Mrs. White is on the hunt for a new dish. We'll be given something egregious for dinner."

"What can we do?" His fingers pattered on the leather Bible clutched to his chest.

She thought for a moment. "Assemble the guests. Suggest we dine out. Perhaps John Boddy would take us to visit one of his cronies in Winchester."

"Excellent solution. I'll seek out the gentlemen if you'll find your daughter. And we'd have to tell Mrs. White. It wouldn't be fair to walk out and leave her holding a hot dish."

Mrs. Peacock allowed a little pout to crease her face. "Why don't you look after all of it, Mr. Green? I'm sure you've had practice organizing dinners for the less fortunate souls. And being victim to one of Mrs. White's new culinary creations certainly makes us less fortunate." She left him standing with the books and disappeared along the passageway.

So, he had a mission. Find Colonel Mustard, Professor Plum, and Mr. Boddy to advise them of the change of plans. Find Miss Scarlet, since Mrs. Peacock did not seem eager to talk to her own daughter. Lastly, find Mrs. White, when the arrangements were made and she couldn't avert the exodus. Where would he find them? He'd wander the passageways until he heard voices.

He found Miss Scarlet in the hall chatting to Mr. Boddy, who was adjusting the front door knocker with a wrench.

"Look what I've got, John," Miss Scarlet said, waving a piece of paper at him. "A letter from the Royal Household inviting me to spend a week at Balmoral Castle in August. I'm ever so thrilled. I'll be the guest of the Prince of Wales. Do you know he's the most eligible bachelor in England?"

Mr. Boddy stopped tinkering and read the letter she thrust at his hands.

Mr. Green watched her dancing around the hall, crimson chiffon frock twirling. "You ought not to blot your copybook between now and then," he said. "The Royal Family is most particular. Blessed are they who stay out of the papers, for they are above public reproach."

"How could I get into trouble at this lonely mansion? There's nobody here but old codgers. I'll have to send an acceptance by the afternoon post. Do you have a pen and some paper, John?"

Old codger? Mr. Green bit back a retort. He was only fifty-four. He was nowhere near a codger. John Boddy was twenty-nine. How tactless of her to insult the host.

Mr. Boddy said nothing, just returned the letter to her anxious fingers and went about his task, the wrench clenched with white knuckles and his lips set in a thin line.

This was perhaps not the most opportune moment to mention the proposed change in dinner plans, if he hoped Mr. Boddy might foot the bill. He'd seek out the others.

He found Professor Plum in the conservatory, peering through his magnifying glass at the leaves of the philodendron. "News, Professor. Mrs. White has been searching through all the cookbooks in the house. We think we ought to dine out."

Professor Plum's glasses slid down his nose. "Sorry, I don't quite follow."

Mr. Green returned to the room door, grasped it by the knob, and wafted it back and forth to create a breeze. "What do you smell, Professor?"

Professor Plum sniffed the air. "Pungent. Fetid. Rancid. Burning."

"Right. That's our dinner. What do you say to a walk down to the local pub for fish and chips?"

Professor Plum fumbled his magnifying glass into his pocket. "Oh, I say, that's rather enticing. I'd love a good meal. How much would it cost, do you think? I'm a bit tight for cash at the moment. I lost my position at the British Museum, you see. I'm waiting for another offer. There's sure to be one forthcoming, but, until then. . . ." His voice trailed off and he sniffed the air again.

"Mr. Boddy might be successfully tapped for the meal. If not, Mrs. Peacock is swimming in money. We'll see if she would treat us. Blessed are the wealthy, for they shall have many friends."

Professor Plum grinned. "That would be capital. I should be delighted to dine out."

Mr. Green left him flipping through the daily paper searching for the solution to yesterday's crossword. Where would he find Colonel Mustard? He checked the billiard room. Empty. He checked the library. John Boddy stood at the table of open recipe books, reading, turning pages. No need to explain the situation to him, then. He'd been eating Mrs. White's culinary fabrications for years.

He carried on to the lounge. Miss Scarlet prattled to a stone-faced Mrs. Peacock about her fabulous offer from the Prince of Wales. Not a good moment to ask a lady for cash.

Back to the original mission. Where would he find Colonel Mustard? In the kitchen? He peeked around the kitchen door. Mrs. White stood at the counter pounding something grey and slimy with a lead pipe. "Getting an early start on dinner, Mrs. White? Perhaps we can save you the trouble."

"I'm testing recipes. I'm entering the recipe competition at the World's Fair in Philadelphia. I read all about it in *The Guardian*. It has to be my own recipe, so I'm starting with a printed recipe that looks good, and making a few substitutions to personalize it. You'll be able to tell me which dish is best tonight at dinner. I've got several on the hop."

Mr. Green cast a lingering look over the shredded brown heap in one bowl, the malodorous bubbling pot on the Aga cooker, and the chopped grey puddle of slime. Swallowing, he tried to fill his mind with thoughts of other cheerful non-edible things, like money or diamonds.

He moved on to the ballroom. Ah-ha, the colonel snored on the gold brocade divan.

"Excuse me, Colonel?"

"Harrumph, what? Oh, Green, it's you. Must have nodded off for a moment. Warm in here. Odd smell, though. Are the drains backed up?"

"Sad to say, that's our dinner. Blessed are those that hunger, for they shall not be ill from eating."

Colonel Mustard sniffed the air again. "That'd take the shoes off your horse. Do you suppose we ought to hope for mashed potatoes on the side?"

"We're rather thinking we ought to dine out. I thought you might be the man to approach Mrs. Peacock about footing the bill. It would be most generous of her to take our host, and ourselves, to dinner."

Colonel Mustard stood and smoothed his uniform. "Dine out. Capital idea. Just the ticket. On Mrs. Peacock's pound? Capital."

"Let's go and find her then, shall we?" Mr. Green said. "She was last seen in the lounge."

Together they strolled down the passageway. They met Professor Plum coming out of the library.

"I say, I was looking for the afternoon papers, so I could work the crossword puzzle. They ought to have been delivered by now. Mrs. White usually takes them from the hall to the library."

"As you can tell by the smoke, she's busy in the kitchen." Mr. Green said. "We were on our way to see Mrs. Peacock about that other matter."

Professor Plum fell in with them.

They found the ladies in the lounge, Mrs. Peacock in one of the green leather chairs reading, and Miss Scarlet slouched on the chintz chesterfield staring at the ornate stucco ceiling.

"Gentlemen. I assume you've come to a consensus concerning the evening's repast?" Mrs. Peacock asked.

"We have, we're all in agreement, except for one small detail." Mr. Green drifted backwards, leaving Colonel Mustard in the firing line.

"We wonder, dear lady, if you would be so kind as to act as hostess for the evening. Someone ought to. Can't think of anyone more well-positioned." Colonel Mustard's moustache quivered.

Mrs. Peacock rose. "Hostess? You mean, will I pay for this dinner for all of you? You can jolly well all pay for your own meals. I'm not made of money."

Miss Scarlet leaped up. "Going out for dinner? Are we? How marvelous. But you'll pay for my meal, won't you, Mother? Please? I've absolutely nothing in my pockets and I need several new frocks to wear at Balmoral."

Mrs. Peacock clenched her jaw and stalked out of the room. Miss Scarlet chased after her. They could hear her pleading voice echoing down the passageway.

"That's that, then," Professor Plum said. "I'm at the mercy of Mrs. White. You all go ahead and have a good time."

"Nonsense, can't leave you behind, old boy. We'll see if Boddy wants to be host. He'll be in the study." Colonel Mustard turned smartly and marched in the direction of the study.

Mr. Green thought he'd be happier letting the Colonel do the dirty work unassisted. He sat down in his favorite green leather armchair.

"Steady on, chaps," Colonel Mustard shouted from the hall. "Boddy's on the floor. Looks a mite pale."

Mr. Green hurried into the hall, with the Professor on his heels. He pushed past the Colonel and knelt down beside Mr. Boddy. "Pale? He's dead. I'd say this wrench must have something to do with his condition."

"The afternoon post has been delivered," Professor Plum observed. "Here's the paper. Would anyone mind if I just tuck this under my arm for later?"

"Clear the area, chaps. I shall go to the study and ring up the authorities." Colonel Mustard pointed to the door and Professor Plum obligingly left the hall gripping the paper. The colonel advanced into the study.

Mr. Green took the opportunity to frisk Mr. Boddy and purloin his wallet. He flipped through the cash as he tucked it into his inner pocket. There was enough here to send four hungry men out to dinner. He replaced the wallet in Mr. Boddy's pocket.

A few moments later Mr. Green stood beside Professor Plum in the lounge.

"What ought we to do next?" Professor Plum asked.

"I'd say you ought to be seeking funding, for we will certainly dine out tonight. The house will be in turmoil once the authorities arrive. We'll need to make ourselves scarce. Blessed are those who need money, for they shall not be frowned upon when they find it. Might I suggest you look under the cushions of the chesterfield for loose change?"

Professor Plum grinned. "Oh, I say, what a corker of an idea." He turned to the furniture and began flipping cushions.

Mr. Green watched his progress for a moment. The man must be flat broke to resort to crawling on his hands and knees around the lounge furniture. He ought to take pity on the poor soul. Blessed are the merciful. He slipped a pound note out of his new-found windfall and jammed it behind the cushion of the closest chair.

"Any luck, Professor?"

"I've found sixpence, a shilling, and a letter." Professor Plum tossed the envelope on the table and moved to the next cushion.

Mr. Green picked up the letter. It was on Tudor Hall stationary, was addressed to the Prince of Wales, and was sealed with red wax bearing the Black family crest. He slid it into his pocket and drifted out of the room.

He found some privacy in the library. Before he could slit open the envelope, a pair of high heels tapped into the room. He ought to say something nice, to show all was forgiven after her refusal to stand for the dinner bill. "I've solved the mystery of the cookbooks, Mrs. Peacock," he said. "Mrs. White is entering a recipe contest at The Philadelphia World's Fair."

"And we're to eat the experiments for dinner." Mrs. Peacock leaned over the open books. "How bad can it be, if she's using actual recipes? Oh, these are Margaret's recipe books. From Boston."

"Margaret's?"

"John Boddy's mother. She moved to Boston when she married Samuel Boddy. I stayed with her for several weeks in 1899. Samuel was a charmer. Margaret cooked some delightful dishes from these recipes. Here's one. *Mrs. Lincoln's Boston Cook Book*. See, she made notes in the margin. *Too much flour. Add more butter.*"

"It sounds like she learned to cook in Mrs. White's kitchen." He looked at the handwritten notes in *The Enterprising Housekeeper*. There were some references to sugar and cinnamon, then on the next page: *Patricia gone Tuesday noon to four. Samuel gone Tuesday all day. I knew it. How could she, my friend?*

"What's all the commotion in the hall?" Mrs. Peacock's hat feathers twitched.

"Something about our choice of dinner location, I think."

"If we're dining out, I'll choose the venue. One can never trust the hoi-polloi with important decisions." She hurried off.

In her absence, he opened the sealed envelope. The letter was addressed to the Prince of Wales and explained that information had recently come to light indicating Mrs. Patricia Peacock, mother of Miss Josephine Scarlet, had been involved in clandestine business with Samuel Boddy, husband of Margaret Boddy, mother of John Boddy. These allegations would be brought to the attention of the tabloids at the earliest convenience.

Mr. Green pocketed the letter and strolled off to the lounge, where he was positive Colonel Mustard would have corralled the troops pending further instructions.

He stopped on the Oriental rug. "I accuse you of killing Mr. Boddy in the hall with the wrench."

RECIPE
FOR
DISASTER

SOLUTION:

"Oh, I say, I found a pound note on that chair. I'll be able to dine out several times. What did you say, Mr. Green?"

"I said, Miss Scarlet killed Mr. Boddy. He found out some lurid details about her mother and his father, and he was going to tell the Prince of Wales."

Mrs. Peacock waved a dismissive hand. "That's ancient history."

"Not to the tabloids, when they find out the daughter of this lady is going to visit the Prince of Wales this summer."

Miss Scarlet crossed her arms. "He had a letter all written. He was waiting for the afternoon post. I had to stop him. They would have rescinded my invitation to Balmoral. Queen Mary is most particular."

Bustling footsteps marched into the room. "This is a fine how-do-you-do," Mrs. White said. "All those recipe books in the library and I can't get at them. The policeman won't let me in."

"I'm sure there are other recipes in the house, Mrs. White," Mrs. Peacock said. "You must have a store of them in the kitchen."

"Right enough, but they're the usual old thing, mutton stew and sheep's head broth. I've need of a foreign dish for an international cooking competition at the World's Fair. Patina of Sole with Herb Sauce. Or Stuffed Squid Fried in Honey."

Mrs. Peacock paled. "Mrs. White, the World's Fair this year is in Philadelphia. To the Americans, England is a foreign country. You make a divine roast beef. Why not submit the recipe for that?"

"There's no recipe for roast beef. You just pop a slab of meat in the Aga cooker and come back a few hours later. Any fool can make a roast of beef."

"What about your scones? They are most delectable, as you can tell from how quickly they vanish at elevenses. I'm sure I've never tasted better. That would be a fine recipe to submit."

Mrs. White balled her hands into fists and placed them on her hips. She stiffened up from head to toe. "I'll have you know, Mrs. Peacock, that my scone recipe has been a secret in the Chaulkley family for six generations. I'm not about to divulge it for the sake of winning a contest. I have my pride."

With that she stomped out of the room.

A Gift
Horse

IN THE DINING ROOM

Mrs. White ladled out plates of oxtail stew and lima beans. Would this suit the guests, or would she be scraping plates later? She'd worked for hours on this stew, and it had been tricky, finding a suitable substitution for onions. Last season's Brussels sprouts were dried and shrunken, like onions. Mayhap they'd impart a similar flavor.

Professor Plum took out his magnifying glass, peered through it, and removed a hair from his stew. "Bovine," he said, placing it on the table beside him.

Mrs. Peacock sighed, but her voice sounded cheerful. "Have you given any thought to what you'll be serving for John Boddy's birthday dinner, Mrs. White? You'll want to make it special."

"Roast beef and Yorkshire pudding, that's the ticket," Colonel Mustard said. "Can't go wrong."

"With a rice pudding for dessert," Mr. Green said. "Without the raisins. Blessed are the easily-recognized ingredients, for they are without suspicion."

"Rice pudding?" Miss Scarlet said. "Whoever heard of rice pudding for dessert at a birthday party? We have to have a birthday cake. We ought to send to the baker in the village for one, with all the fancy icing and John's name on it."

"Truth to tell, I've not given the matter much thought, although I like the notion of ordering a cake," Mrs. White said. "Have you all decided what you'll be giving him for a birthday gift?"

No one answered. Much attention was paid to the stew, the cutlery, and the view out the window. Mrs. White shrugged. As she suspected, not a thought for anyone but themselves.

The door opened. John Boddy meandered in with a patina of gloom in his eyes.

"There you are, Mr. Boddy, and a lovely dinner it is tonight," Mrs. Peacock said with forced gaiety. "The lima beans are perfection."

IN THE LOUNGE

Later that evening, Miss Scarlet sat close to Mrs. Peacock on the chintz chesterfield. "What are we going to get John for his birthday?"

"We? You can get him whatever you want. I am not going to buy a gift and add your name to it."

"Mother, please, I've no money, you know that."

"You've money enough to spend on yourself. Why not take back that new handbag you just acquired and use the refund to buy him some little thing."

"Oh, Mother." Miss Scarlet sat back on the chesterfield with a sigh. How could she return the handbag? She'd pinched it. That could be the answer. She'd find a nice silver picture frame, tuck it under her coat and slip out of the shop. Insert a photo of herself, one of her acting photos. Still it was rather mean of Mother not to share. How could she sit there wearing four strands of pearls and not spare three shillings to her own daughter in a time of need?

IN THE LIBRARY

Professor Plum flipped through the books on the top and bottom shelves of the library. Birthday gift, birthday gift. If he found an insignificant book, he could take it to the village used book shop and swap it for another. It wasn't really stealing. It was a fair exchange. No one would miss one of these books, judging by the cobwebs in the far corners. What could he choose as a gift for Mr. Boddy? A book of crossword puzzles would be ideal. He'd be trading a book no one read for a book Mr. Boddy could use. That would be an overall improvement. Yes. Not like stealing at all.

IN THE BILLIARD ROOM

"Any ideas, Green, about a gift for Boddy?" Colonel Mustard asked. "Slipped my mind."

Mr. Green picked up a billiard cue and began chalking the tip. It had slipped his mind, too, but here he was in a mansion full of knick knacks. It was simply a matter of finding something dusty in the back corner of a cupboard, brushing it off, and putting it in a box. "No ideas at all. I suppose something for the house, as he's the home owner."

"I rather thought something more personal, like a pocket watch or a riding crop. Dash it all, I've not the scratch to visit the shops. Can you spare a few shillings, Green?"

"I'm up against it myself. My pockets are nearly flat. Would you care to play a little billiards? Let's say for a shilling? That would give the winner two shillings to spend."

Colonel Mustard leaned his riding crop against the cue rack. "You're on."

IN THE KITCHEN

Mrs. White flipped through her favorite recipe book. Those guests and their feeble ideas. Imagine serving roast beef and Yorkshire pudding to Master Boddy on his birthday. She served that every week. She needed something special. The idea of sending out to the bake shop for cake appealed to her. Save all that work fussing with icing roses and colored lettering. Come to think of it, she ought to hire out the entire meal. How much would it cost?

She pulled out the household account book. Her monthly kitchen allowance was depleted, most of it spent on a tartan shawl for chilly evenings. Never mind. She would ring up the local restaurant, ask if they could make up a birthday meal, and ask how much it would cost. She'd double their figure, write out a bill for this amount for Master Boddy and tell him it was for unexpected added expenses brought on by having house guests. He'd open the wall safe and count out the money.

She'd have enough to pay for the meal and buy him a gift. The remainder would go in her secret retirement account.

Now, what to buy the master of the house for his birthday? A silver soup ladle would be perfect.

LATER THE NEXT DAY IN THE KITCHEN

"I say, Mrs. White, do you have a carrot or an apple?" Professor Plum held out a hand at the kitchen door.

"A bit peckish, are we? Shall I peel and slice it for you?"

"No, no, whole is fine. One of each, if you have them. Two of each if you can spare them. Thank you." Professor Plum took his beggings and hurried out the rear door.

IN THE LOUNGE

"My pearls are missing, Josephine. Do you have any idea where they might be?" Mrs. Peacock asked.

"How could I, Mother? You never let me wear them. Have you looked under your dresser?"

"I investigated every inch of my room. They're gone."

"Perhaps Mrs. White pinched them, while she was making your bed."

"Why would she do that? She has no occasion to wear pearls."

"She might, to an upcoming birthday party."

Mrs. Peacock frowned. Josephine was involved, somehow, with the missing pearls. However, she wasn't the craftiest of thieves. One only had to wait for her to blunder.

Now, on to the next problem, finding a gift for John Boddy. One of her late husband Sir Matthew Peacock's law books would do. Impressive and useless. She'd ring the law office and have one sent around.

IN THE GARDEN

"I say, Mr. Green, this is more difficult than it looks," Professor Plum said. "Could you stop him from going around to the front of the house? I don't want Mr. Boddy to see him. It's his birthday present, you see."

"A horse? You bought him a horse? That thing is gigantic. Feet like tree stumps. However did you manage, Professor?"

"He was quite a bargain. But I'm trying to keep him hidden in the stables until the birthday, and the wretched thing keeps slipping the latch and getting out."

"I suppose he's hungry. Blessed are the hungry, for they shall dine on the pastures of green."

"I've been feeding him carrots and apples. What more could he want?"

"Cabbages, by the looks of things. And beans, and lettuce and beets and peas. Oops, not the rhubarb, not to his taste."

"Oh, I say, Mrs. White will be livid if she finds he's eaten all her garden."

"Trampled it, too. Good luck to you, Professor."

"Don't leave me, please don't leave. Here, horsey, come here. Nice horsey. Come to Papa Plum and have a nice apple. Oh, no, not the roses."

IN THE HALL

"What's the matter with Master Boddy?" Mrs. White asked. "Why is he lying on the floor?"

"Looks like he's come a cropper," Colonel Mustard replied. "Stand clear. Wrench is the culprit, I should say. Saw him earlier, tampering with the armor, tightening the joints." Colonel Mustard reached out with his riding crop. "What's all this, then? A bank book and a pawn ticket?" He picked them up and studied them.

Mrs. White frowned. "I suppose that's the end of the birthday party."

Colonel Mustard stroked his moustache. "Indeed."

Well, how fortunate for him. He'd lost six shillings to Mr. Green at billiards, and had been on the verge of wrapping up his own pocket watch as a gift, hoping Boddy wouldn't notice the inscription *Meritorious Service – The Sudan.*

IN THE CONSERVATORY

"I suppose you're wondering why I've gathered you all together." Colonel Mustard drew himself to attention under the Bismarck palm.

"To tell us a war story?" Miss Scarlet guessed. "I'm not listening unless you tell us what they were wearing."

"No, to tell you the birthday party is off. Boddy is dead. Clobbered with a wrench. The authorities will be here to look after things soon. We must keep clear of the hall." Colonel Mustard placed two objects on the edge of the stone fountain. "I found these beside the body. A pawn ticket and a bank book. Does anyone lay claim to either?"

"Dead? Is he now?" Mrs. Peacock ruffled her feathers. "I accuse you of killing Boddy in the hall with the wrench."

A GIFT HORSE

SOLUTION:

Miss Scarlet stamped her foot. "I did not. Just because your pearls are missing, you think I'm to blame for everything that goes wrong."

"Did you let Professor Plum's horse out, too?" Mr. Green asked.

"What horse? I don't know anything about a horse," Miss Scarlet said.

"The horse Professor Plum bought to give Boddy as a birthday gift." Mr. Green said. "I suppose you won't be needing him now, Professor. Will you get your money back, do you suppose?"

"I rather think not. You see, I didn't actually buy it. The thing just happened along, wandering down the lane. I found him on my way to the village shops. So I thought, a horse is a good gift. I think Boddy liked to ride."

Mr. Green pointed to the hairy rump framed by the window. "There's that horse again, in the ornamental shrubs. Hop to it, Professor. Blessed are the fast of foot, for they shall not need to ride."

Mrs. White leaped to the window. "That's not a riding horse, that's a flaming Clydesdale. Look what he's done to my herb garden!"

"I'm sorry, I can't make him do as he's told," Professor Plum said. "Would you like to keep him, Mrs. White, as compensation for the damage he's caused?"

"Me? A Clydesdale?" Mrs. White threw up her hands. "I wonder if some homicidal tramp was riding that horse up the lane. Perhaps he stopped at the door to ask for a handout and killed Boddy. By the time he left the house, the horse had wandered off, so he ran away. The horse came back later."

Colonel Mustard nodded. "Seems a likely story. We'll go with that, then, shall we? Homicidal tramp? Lost horse?"

Mr. Green nodded. He'd wrapped up a nice ivory finger bowl, but he could unwrap it and put it back in the billiard room behind the trophies where he'd found it.

Mrs. Peacock nodded. She only needed to find a moment to ring through to the law office and tell them not to bother with the book. She had no idea where her pearls were, but the pawn ticket was a clue. There must be a way to trick Josephine into fetching them.

Miss Scarlet nodded. She'd have to use some sleight of hand to get the pawn ticket for Mother's pearls back from the Colonel. Or maybe not. If she retrieved the pearls, she'd have to give back the money, and she'd seen a pair of shoes she rather liked.

Professor Plum nodded. Anything to be rid of that horse. With no party, there was no need for gifts. He'd just let the wretch wander away. Maybe toss some apples down the lane to encourage him.

Mrs. White nodded. She'd get the bankbook back when she did up the colonel's room. Trust Master Boddy to actually read the figures and see she'd be skimming from the household accounts. The wrench was handy, so she'd used it.

She'd ring up the fishmonger, tell him Bertrand was wandering again, had eaten up half her garden, and ten pounds of fresh fish would be adequate compensation this time when he came to fetch the beast.

Problems solved.

And she had a nice new silver soup ladle to boot.

POOLED

Miss Scarlet stared out the dining room windows at the extensive lawn and concrete swimming pool.

"More coffee, Miss Scarlet? I'm about to toss the dregs." Mrs. White paused midway between the dining room door and the kitchen, the silver serving tray balanced on one hand while she dusted a candlestick with the other.

"Of course I want more coffee. I can never get enough coffee." She extended her cup in Mrs. White's general direction. "I was just looking at the swimming pool. It's nothing like the outdoor pool at San Simeon. My friend Georgia Peach and I had a brilliant week there. Some film person invited us. That William Randolph Hearst sure knows how to entertain, not that we saw him much, only for dinner. He has this marvelous mansion with two pools. The outdoor pool is especially wonderful. All Greek columns, blue and white tile designs on the pool floor under the water. It's on the top of a mountain, you can see for miles. It was all too thrilling for words."

Mrs. White put her tray down, tucked the duster in her pocket and poured coffee into Miss Scarlet's cup. "I'm sure it was." She paused and tapped her toe on the hardwood. "Are you finished with your cup? I've the dishes to do and lunch to make."

"This pool, by comparison, is quite a disappointment." Miss Scarlet waved her hand at the vista through the window. "A white concrete pool, a grey deck, and a few dozen trees around it. The water is absolutely floating with dead leaves. Doesn't anyone look after the pool?"

"I'm sure I've more to do than rake a pool," Mrs. White said, straightening her white cap. "Nobody swims in it anyway. Sir Hugh swam every day, but he's been dead these twelve years. He was a good swimmer, he was. Pity he drowned. Master Boddy swam with him when he was a boy. After he'd gone away to college, he didn't spend much time here. He's done a little swimming every summer since he took over the place in 1918. Not this summer, though. Busy, I expect, planning his birthday party."

Miss Scarlet frowned at the dingy scene. It matched her dingy spirits, drooping inch by inch since her arrival. She was nearly driven mad with boredom. "We ought to have a pool party. That would be spot-on. I could invite some of my friends." They would be much livelier than this bunch of old fossils.

"A party? I'm sure I've enough to do preparing for the big birthday party. I've not time to fuss with invitations."

"Oh, I'll do that. I'll ask John if I can invite some people for a few days. They'll be gone before his birthday party. That's nearly two weeks away."

Mrs. White inclined her head at the windows. "I've not time to clean up the pool, either."

"I'll see to that. I'll see to everything. Don't worry at all, Mrs. White. I'll prepare the entire party myself."

Mrs. White sniffed and took Miss Scarlet's coffee cup, placing it on her silver tray. "As like as naught," she said, and disappeared through the kitchen door.

Miss Scarlet marched out the side door to the pool and stood on the pool deck. First, she'd need to get someone to clean up the water. The water in Hearst's pool was a glittery blue. This pool was murky, not appealing at all. Neither was the décor. Maybe she could get those trees stripped of their branches and painted white, like Greek columns. And paint the concrete pool deck white with a blue Greek design. Oh, and gold leaf highlights. Dozens of deck chairs, tons of tables, fluffy white bathing towels. Tall colorful drinks and canapés served by liveried footmen. Guests bringing her gifts. It would be a smashing party.

Where to start?

She ought to start by clearing the leaves out of the pool. The little building near the pool deck might hold the appropriate tool. She opened the narrow door. Indeed, it was full of all kinds of interesting implements. She picked out a net on a long handle and started scooping leaves out of the water. After three scoops her pinky finger drew a sliver from the wooden handle, and she had to stop.

"What ho, Miss Scarlet, wrong tool for the job." Colonel Mustard strode toward her from the driveway, swinging his riding crop. His medals glowed in a neat line across the chest of his uniform. "That's a fishing net. Sir Hugh and I did a spot of fishing in Scotland now and again. Stored the gear here in the off season. We were fishing when he died. Dashed awkward affair, that. No end of confusion. You'll want a pool skimmer for that job. Let's see what we have in here."

He positioned himself at the open door of the tiny shed. "Try this." He handed her a net with a tighter weave and a longer handle. "If you're trying to get the pool operational, you'll need to attend to that circulating pump. It ought to be running, once you've cleared out the debris." He pointed to a piece of machinery inside the shed.

"Here, you fix it then," she said, plucking a wrench from a shelf and thrusting it into his hands. "You ought to understand motors."

She ducked out before he could protest and hurried back to her skimming job. This net was much more efficient. She collected three whole scoops of leaves before she needed to stop for a rest. Really, the pool was in such a state, with big clods of black gunk lurking over the drains. She couldn't possibly touch those, not even with a long stick.

"I say, Miss Scarlet, are you planning on swimming?" Professor Plum asked, trotting across the grass with a newspaper tucked under his arm. "Lovely day for it."

"I thought I might hold a pool party. Invite some of my friends."

"That does sound jolly. Anything I can do to help? Give you a list of my friends to invite, perhaps?"

"You might help me with the pool cleanup. Scoop up some floating leaves." She shoved the net in his free hand and darted back to the shed. Colonel Mustard was gone, with the wrench, and the pump looked no more operational than a broken movie camera. She returned to Professor Plum with a lead pipe. "There seems to be something stuck in the drain thingy in this corner. Try whacking the drain with this."

She reclaimed her net, pushed the pipe into Professor Plum's hands, and ignored his shocked expression. He gazed at the tool in his hand for a moment, and his purple bow tie actually wilted. He got down on one knee and poked at the black sludge with the lead pipe.

Good. He was helping. Miss Scarlet walked to the deep end of the pool and snagged another scoop of leaves. She didn't want to be close to Professor Plum when he cleared the drain, as the sludge was apt to be stinky.

"Whatever are you doing, Josephine?" Mrs. Peacock's voice echoed from the dining room door. She came wandering out to the pool deck carrying a candlestick. "I've been looking for you, to ask if you thought this was Louis Quatorze or Louis Quinze."

"However should I know, Mother? I didn't know candlesticks had names. Listen, I'm planning a pool party, and I want to invite all my friends. Would you write the invitations for me? You're so good at that sort of thing."

"No, I most certainly will not. I sent you to Miss Puce's School for Girls so you would learn how to hostess parties, among other things. Did you not pay any attention at all?" She stalked back to the house, her sapphire silk frock sparking warnings in the sunlight.

Miss Scarlet looked back at the pool. Professor Plum was gone. The drain still looked plugged. Drat. No one would help. This party was becoming a colossal nightmare of jobs to be done. She attacked the water with the net, scooping four large batches of leaves before she broke into a light sweat and had to stop. She slumped into the closest deck chair. This task was impossible. She could not continue alone. She had only two people left to ask, that odious Mr. Green, and John Boddy.

Of course, John Boddy. He'd help. It was his pool. He knew how to run the pump and clean the drains. He knew how to write invitations, too. The invitation he'd sent for his upcoming birthday party had been exquisite.

She dropped her net on the concrete, and rose from her chair. John was watching her through the dining room window. She waved. He waved back. She noticed a flutter in the air behind him, and John fell forward, his face splayed on the window glass.

As she watched, he slid slowly down until he disappeared below the window ledge.

How very odd. But at least she knew where he was. She began a slow stroll toward the house, so he'd have an extended time to admire her beauty shimmering in the sunlight. When she reached the door she glanced at her reflection in the window. Raspberry red blouse and skirt, with a silver locket and freshly curled hair. Perfect. John would be unable to refuse her slightest wish.

If she made a dramatic entrance into the dining room, swept the double doors open and paused so her silhouette could be framed by the rich mahogany, she could ask him for anything.

She executed the dramatic entrance perfectly. She expected him to turn from the windows with a half smile on his face, his eyes lit up in anticipation of her company.

Instead she found him slumped on the floor at the windows, a big dent in his head that could only have been inflicted by a blunt object.

The dining room table was in disarray, with the place settings pushed to one side, leaving a large clear spot. An empty file folder lay near Boddy's hand. She touched his shoulder, and he rolled to one side. A yellowed bit of paper protruded from his breast pocket. She slipped it into her own pocket.

What to do now? Call the Colonel. He might not be good at motors, but he was good at bossing people around.

In no time Colonel Mustard was barking orders and blocking the door to the dining room while he awaited the arrival of the authorities. As the others collected around him, demanding to know what was going on, the policemen arrived, issuing instructions and asking questions.

Miss Scarlet tiptoed away to John's study and closed the door. She curled up on the red leather desk chair and rested her chin on her knees. John had been murdered. And unless she was mistaken, she'd seen it happen. Really! She, Miss Josephine Scarlet, age 25, had seen a murder. It would be in all the papers. Theatre companies would be clamoring for her in lead roles. Oh dear. The policemen had said none of them could leave the mansion until they had discovered the culprit. She'd miss all the auditions if this wasn't sorted soon. Plus she'd have to cancel her pool party.

Well, then, she'd have to solve it herself.

What had she seen from the poolside? Nothing, really, just a blur in the shadows of the room's interior.

What had she seen when she found him in the dining room? She squeezed her eyes shut and thought hard. A gap on the table. Why would the table settings be pushed aside? Everyone knew Mrs. White did not like her table messed about. An empty file folder. Why would a file folder be empty? Because the papers had been spread out on the table. Ah-ha, now she was getting somewhere. This sleuthing business was simple. If her acting career didn't work out, she could become a detective. She'd swoop into a crime scene, glance about, proclaim the solution, and sweep out of the room. They'd pay her extra for rapid solutions. She could solve three or four crimes a day, and be home by teatime.

Where was she? Oh, yes, papers in a file folder. Papers taken from the folder and spread on the table. They weren't on the table when she found the body. Why was that? Had they blown away in the breeze when she opened the door? No, they'd still be in the room, flapping in the corners. There were no papers loose in the dining room. Ah-ha, that meant the papers were now missing.

Her objective ought to be to find the lost papers. What kind of papers? Bills, letters, recipes—something John had that the killer wanted. Mrs. White's secret recipe for scones? No, even John didn't have access to that. She ought to look for the papers. It was a good thing the killer had missed one. She pulled the fragment of old paper from her pocket. It was a newspaper clipping.

Sir Hugh Black died this week in a tragic fishing accident. Sir Hugh had been fishing in Scotland when his feet became entangled in fishing line. He leaves behind a nephew, John Boddy, and a wife, the former Mrs. Patricia Gobelin Scarlet Zaffer. The widow was unavailable for comment according to her solicitor, Sir Matthew Peacock.

She sat up and read the clipping again. Mother was married to Sir Hugh? Then the mansion belonged to her, not John Boddy. She and Mother could live here and she could hire someone to clean the pool. Why had Mother never told her about this?

Where would Mother be at this time of day? Hanging about in the kitchen giving Mrs. White orders and trying to get bread and butter on the lunch menu, so they wouldn't all starve.

She'd go there and demand an explanation. On the way she noticed Professor Plum in the library, tucking something between the pages of a book. A little further along the passageway, she noticed Colonel Mustard in the billiard room, pushing something under one of the trophies. She didn't stop to pass the time of day. Mother had deceived her. Mother had concealed her inheritance.

Mother was in the kitchen, as suspected, pointing out something in a recipe book to Mrs. White.

"It says chopped parsley, Mrs. White. You can't substitute turnip and have the recipe turn out the same."

"Don't see why not. I substituted olives for carrots in the mutton pies and they turned out well."

Mrs. Peacock sighed, closed the recipe book, and sucked on the tip of her index finger.

"Excuse me, Mother, I wonder if I could have a word," Miss Scarlet said. "In the ballroom."

Mrs. Peacock followed her to the ballroom and sat on the gold brocade settee near the grand piano. "If you're going to ask me for more money, the answer is no, Josephine."

Miss Scarlet sat beside her and lowered her voice to a whisper. "It has come to my attention, Mother, that you and Sir Hugh were married."

Mrs. Peacock blushed. "Silly girl, where did you get a notion like that?"

"From a newspaper clipping."

"Oh, the papers always get things wrong. You know that." She licked the tip of her finger. "I must get back and see what other hideous things Mrs. White has done with the lunch. We could all starve." She left in a flurry of hat feathers.

Miss Scarlet pulled the newspaper clipping out of her pocket and reread it. Newspapers did get things wrong, that was true. The newspaper reviewers had called her last performance banal, and that was definitely untrue. Still, Mother had been known to tell a fib or two when it suited her needs. Maybe she should ask Mrs. White. She's worked for Sir Hugh before John Boddy inherited the mansion. She'd know if Sir Hugh ever married anyone.

In the passageway, Colonel Mustard stood guard at the dining room, even though the authorities had the door closed and possibly locked. His at-attention pose leaned on the gilt frame of an ancestral portrait.

"Still at it, are they?" she asked, not really wanting a reply.

He straightened up, and the painting rocked on the wall. "They are. Reminds me of the time Sir Hugh died, all the careful attention to detail.

They've asked me the same questions three times now, as they did then. I remember that day clearly. Sir Hugh, Mrs. White, Mrs. Peacock and I were holidaying in the Highlands." Colonel Mustard rocked back on his heels and got a far-away look in his eyes "Well, Mrs. Zaffer she was then."

Oh dear, he was launching into a war story. Except Mother was in this one. Perhaps she ought to listen.

"I remember I'd just finished a stint with the signals corps and was waiting reassignment. We'd set up a command post in a cottage, and settled in for a fortnight. We were going fishing, Sir Hugh and I, while I was between postings."

Between postings. In acting circles they called it between parts, and it meant out of work. Was he broke, too, like she was every time she was between engagements?

"We'd gone to one of our favorite spots on the River Spean near Ben Nevis. The river rushes through a high narrow spot, down a waterfall, then widens into a deep pool. Bit of a current, swirly, but a fine spot for casting. Crisp day, early morning, just the ticket for a fine catch. We'd hiked along the path beside the river. I was in the lead, setting the pace. Sir Hugh followed. He was the same age as myself but not as spry at 50 as I, having lived a more sedentary life of finances, while I'd been a career soldier and kept fit."

"As you still are." She fluttered her eyelashes, pretending she was completely captivated by his tale, to keep him talking until he got to the part about Mother.

"Thank you, yes, I do keep up. Walking, you know, does the heart good. As I was saying, I'd just set down my tackle when I heard a noise, a high-pitched shout. I didn't see anything at first, but then I saw the heels of Sir Hugh's hip waders in the water. He'd waded out a bit too far, stepped in a deep section, and lost his balance. His waders filled with water and pulled him under. There was nothing I could do. Don't swim, you see. Mrs. Zaffer came running along as fast as her wellies would allow, but by that time he'd disappeared. We didn't find him until the next day, battered by the rocks and drowned. Tragedy."

"A tragedy, yes. Much like today's tragedy."

"I recall another tragedy. We were stationed in Cairo, hoping to be sent on to Rangoon. It was dark; you could hardly see your gun in your hand."

Miss Scarlet glanced at her wrist. "Oh dear, the time, I must be off." She hurried away. One of these days she ought to buy a watch. Where was she? Oh yes, asking Mrs. White if Sir Hugh and Mother had been married. In the conservatory she found Mrs. White setting knives and forks on small tables around the room. The fish in the tank regarded her with suspicion.

"They won't let me have my dining room, you know, so you'll have to eat lunch in here." Mrs. White said. "Bit of a nuisance, with spider plants hanging over the plates."

Miss Scarlet ran a finger along a philodendron leaf. She ought to ease into her question. Start with some innocuous chatter. "Even if they did let us eat in there, the dining table is a mess, with place settings pushed to one side."

"What? Have they messed about with my table?" Mrs. White brandished a knife in the direction of the dining room.

"Actually, I think it was John Boddy who messed it about. I think he had some papers spread out on it."

Mrs. White sighed. "How many times did I tell him, if you want to show some papers to someone, do it in the study, or in the library, there's tables in there."

"There were no papers on the dining table."

"Someone's taken them, then. Good thing. I shall be able to put the table right when the authorities have gone."

Miss Scarlet smiled. Verification of her own thoughts. The file folder had contained papers, which John had spread on the table, and those papers were missing. Now she could ask the important question. Ask Mrs. White about weddings.

But Mrs. White had gone back to the kitchen and sounds of pots clanging echoed through the passageways. Perhaps this was not the best time to ask her more questions. She'd have to set the wedding problem aside. Move on to the next line of investigation. Find the missing papers. How do you find papers in a house full of papers? She mulled that over as she walked down the passageway to the billiard room and library. Oh, right, she'd seen two people hiding papers earlier. She ought to steal them.

Mr. Green leaned on a cue in the billiard room, contemplating his next move. Miss Scarlet edged into the room and positioned herself in front of the trophy cabinet. "Filling in the time, Mr. Green?" she asked. He was looking particularly drab today, in moss green trousers and olive green jacket. He looked like a dark day in the woods.

"Indeed, as a man of the cloth I shall have work to do by tomorrow, consoling the mourners over the passing of a loved one. Blessed are the ordained, for they shall be paid for their sympathy. I am marshalling my thoughts by performing a mindless activity."

"I didn't think billiards was mindless." She ran her fingers on the shelf behind her until they contacted paper.

"Normally it is an intellectual game of skill, but sometimes, when playing alone, its repetition calms the inner turmoil." He chalked his cue with damp pudgy fingers.

"I see. Well, I'll leave you to it. I don't want to be the cause of lingering turmoil." She pulled the papers from their hiding place and palmed them until she had retreated from the room. And Mother thought she hadn't learned anything useful at Miss Puce's School for Girls. In the passageway, she tucked the booty in to her pocket while pretending to admire a Ming vase.

The library was empty. Professor Plum was gone, the reading table abandoned save for one slender grey volume. She searched for a book containing a slip of paper. After unsuccessfully shaking out an entire row of books from the first shelf, she sat down at the reading table. Four separate bookcases. A whole room full of books. How could she find the right one? Why couldn't it be as easy as, say, picking up a book left on the table, and having it flip open to the errant slip of paper? Oh. It was that easy. The paper fluttered to the table. She picked it up and stuffed it into her pocket.

Now, where to go to read the papers in private?

The study. John wouldn't be using it anymore.

Closing the door behind her, she settled into the red leather chair again and pulled out her secret papers. Drat. She didn't know which was which.

My Dear Friend,

As much as I enjoy your company, I am greatly displeased by the debacle of Gretna Green, and how you could set me up for such folly. Patricia says you're an old mooch and intend to sponge a living off me. I doubt that. She doesn't know you as I do, and such a long association as ours is not taken lightly. To appease her, I've spoken to a friend at the Home Office, and highly recommended you to him. I trust you will be on your way soon.

She couldn't read the scrawly signature.

My Dear Friend,

As much as I enjoy your company, I am greatly displeased by the proposed journey you have outlined in your prospectus. Inasmuch as great scientific discovery is hard won, nevertheless I don't wish it to be won out of the pocket-books of gentlemen such as I. I've spoken to a friend at the British Museum, and highly recommended you to him. I trust you will be on your way soon.

The same scrawly signature ended the note. Both pages seemed to be a record of correspondence, as they were on plain paper. If they had been written on letterhead paper, she might have a clue who wrote them. Letterhead. She'd almost forgotten in her diligent search for the evil-doer. She needed to write invitations to the pool party. John wouldn't need his letterhead anymore, and it was luxurious. She scooped up a big handful from his desk. Using his fine fountain pen, she wrote *Come to my party* on the top sheet. It didn't sound like quite enough, somehow. She'd need Mother to help with the wording.

She gathered a stack of John's Tudor Mansion letterhead, shoved the old letters back in her pocket, and went in search of Mother.

In the passageway near the lounge, she found a bunch of papers scrunched inside a brass spittoon. She paused in the front hall to read them.

My Dear Friend,

As much as I enjoy your company, I must ask you to remain in London and sort out this tangle. Whereas a Captain has legal powers at sea, I doubt an army officer has legal powers on land. I do not consider this a legal and binding arrangement, nor do I see cause to alter my will. I shall not, therefore, be altering the current direction of my estate into the hands of my nephew when he comes of age, regardless of what babble has been rained on your ears of late. I trust you will be on your way soon to a complete settlement of this affair.

This letter did not have a signature, only indecipherable initials. The other papers appeared to be Sir Hugh's will, and a marriage certificate that had been caught in the rain. The former was too long and tedious to read, and the latter unreadable because the ink had bled. No help here.

She could hear Mother in the lounge, going on about something. She tucked the papers back in the spittoon and gripped the stack of letterhead. She paused at the lounge door. Charm and tact, even if it was her own mother.

Mrs. Peacock was reclining on the chintz chesterfield, suggesting words to Professor Plum, who was hunched over the crossword puzzle. "Prevaricate, preternatural, precocious, preservative. Do any of those fit?"

Professor Plum scribbled, shook his head, rubbed out, scribbled again. His purple tweed jacket almost clashed with the green leather chair he sat in.

"Excuse me, Mother, I was wondering if you could help me with these invitations? I've written *Come to my party*, but I think I need a few more words." Miss Scarlet held out the fountain pen and the first sheet of letterhead.

Mrs. Peacock held out her hand to block the advancing pen. "You might consider telling them where and when, and that it's a pool party so they bring the proper attire."

"Mother, you are absolutely brilliant." Miss Scarlet settled herself in the green leather chair opposite Professor Plum and began writing. This could become tedious after the first three. She'd need to jolly Mother around into writing the bulk of them for her. "It's been a dreadful day here, with John dying. It does a person good to do something simple and repetitive, don't you think?"

Professor Plum nodded. "Most assuredly. No, it's not 'pre', it's 'per'. Perfect. That's the word. That fits. Now let's see, three down, fishing term, seven letters."

"Did you ever go fishing, Mother? That's simple and repetitive, much like writing invitations."

Mrs. Peacock narrowed her eyes, like she did when she spotted a trap. "Fishing? Not often. I remember one occasion, when I was holidaying in Scotland, visiting Sir Hugh at his summer cottage. It was a lovely day for a walk in the woods. Sir Hugh had his fishing gear and I had a picnic, and we were going to spend a delightful day by the river. Hugh was leading the way along the path beside the river. I had fallen behind as I'd gotten a stone in my walking shoe and it took a minute to find a suitable rock to sit on, and retie my laces. Hugh had gone out of sight around a bend, and I heard him shout. When I got to the spot at the top of the waterfall, Colonel Mustard was looking down into the pool. I didn't see Hugh anywhere. We hurried down the path and called out to Hugh, but we didn't find him until the next day. It was quite dreadful."

"It didn't turn out to be a fishing trip, then."

"No, more of a fresh air and trouble trip. I came straight home, as soon as the police would allow. That's when I met Sir Matthew Peacock, as a result of the legalities following Sir Hugh's death." Mrs. Peacock turned and gazed out the window, dabbing at the corner of her eye with a blue lace hanky.

Miss Scarlet frowned at her invitations. Mother was feigning distress, she was sure. Sir Matthew had been dead for nine years. Mother's story about the fishing trip was different from Colonel Mustard's tale. How did real detectives manage when they had to sort through conflicting reports? This sleuthing business was too much work, added to the burden of writing the invitations unassisted. She ought to hunt down Mrs. White and cadge a cup of tea and a slice of shortbread to shore up her spirits.

She found Mrs. White in the kitchen, putting together the lunch tray.

"I wonder if there's any tea going, Mrs. White?"

"There will be tea with lunch if you can wait five minutes. It's been a dreadful day, shut out of the dining room and having to make do in the conservatory. Even worse than the day Sir Hugh disappeared."

"Was it this inconvenient when Sir Hugh died?"

"Inconvenient, and more. It were a miserable day, it were, both indoors and out. Sir Hugh was shouting into the telephone about not changing a hair of his will, Mrs. Zaffer was whining about my choice of soup for lunch, and Colonel Mustard found the porridge not to his liking. I'd a mind to clobber them all. I was doing my best under trying circumstances, with a rented six-bedroom cottage and struggling to find the pots and pans. I'd set about making a dilly of a lunch, lima bean soup, kippers and fried bread, with a big pot of tea." She picked up a large teapot and placed it on the tray. "Anyroad, the rain started pelting down, and Sir Hugh said he was going out. Grabbed his walking stick and out the door. Mrs. Zaffer fumed around for a while, then packed on her rain gear and off she went, swinging her brolly. About a half hour later, the sun broke through. Colonel Mustard said he was going fishing, although I thought it was a bit late in the day for fishing, nearly noon it was. An hour later they both came back, and said they'd seen no sign of Sir Hugh. My lunch was ruined by then, the kippers curled up like dry leaves. The colonel said it was all right, he wasn't hungry anyway. Neither was Mrs. Zaffer.

It wasn't until the next day they found Sir Hugh, floating in the pool at the base of the waterfall. They fished out his Italian walking shoes and his pocket watch the day after. Poor lad, and him being a strong swimmer and all."

"And John Boddy his only heir. Had he never been married?"

"Sir Hugh, married? No, he never was, although he had a soft spot for your mother. Almost spoiled a holiday once, she did. Back in my home-land, and me visiting the old haunts and stocking up on Scottish bits and bobs. We'd stopped for tea in Gretna Green. And here she comes with her silly talk about they're being on their honeymoon now, and Colonel Mustard ought to hop it. Right miffed, he was. Said he'd come for a spot of fishing with his old friend, and dash it, that's what he was going to do. Well, I never saw such a palaver as she kicked up in the next few days. On and on about how she was the lady of the house now, and Colonel Mustard had outstayed his welcome, and Sir Hugh better get telephoning his solicitor. One day she placed the call herself, and made Sir Hugh come to speak to the man. He was in a right tear that day. Well, that about fills the tray. You can go and tell the others lunch is ready."

Miss Scarlet watched her carry the heavy tray out of the kitchen. Mother hadn't mentioned the honeymoon thingy. She returned to the lounge.

"Lunch is served in the conservatory. Professor, could you go and tell Colonel Mustard and Mr. Green?"

Professor Plum folded his crossword and tucked it beside the chair cushion. "Indeed. Looking forward to a light nosh."

When he had left the room, Miss Scarlet restrained her mother's arm. "Not so fast, Mother. Mrs. White says the item in the newspaper was true. She says you and Sir Hugh were on your honeymoon."

Mrs. Peacock waved the notion away. "It was tom-foolery, that's all. Playing around at Gretna Green. I said if it was a battlefield, Colonel Mustard could marry us, like a ship's captain can marry you when you're out at sea. Hugh and I exchanged some serious words over the anvil, then we all laughed and went to the closest tea room for cakes with clotted cream. Mrs. White joined us shortly; she'd been shopping for tartan." She glanced down and rubbed the tip of her index finger.

"What's wrong with your finger?" Miss Scarlet asked.

"Nothing, just a little cut." Mrs. Peacock held up the offending finger. It bore a thin white cut about a half inch long. "Let's go and see what atrocity Mrs. White has prepared on our behalf."

They joined the others in the conservatory. Mrs. White was looking pleased with herself. Colonel Mustard was surreptitiously dumping his kipper in a potted plant. Mr. Green and Professor Plum were making tentative pokes with forks at the heap on their plates. Miss Scarlet headed straight for the teapot. That was better. She was absolutely parched with the effort of asking all these questions. She felt very close to the answer, but it eluded her. Drat. She needed this problem out of the way so she could focus on the party invitations. She set her cup on the mantel and rubbed her temples, in case that would stimulate her brain cells.

On the mantel she noticed two gold candlesticks, a silver candlestick, a lead pipe and a wrench. Miss Scarlet stared at the arrangement. One of these objects did not belong. She picked it up and turned to face the group.

"I accuse you of killing John Boddy in the dining room with this."

POOLED

SOLUTION:

Mrs. White plucked it out of her hands. "Don't be daft. That's the candle-stick from the dining room."

"So what's it doing in here? Everyone knows candlesticks are set out in pairs. This one is the odd one on this mantel. There is already a pair there. This one does not belong." She turned to Mrs. Peacock. "You were the one carrying a candlestick when John was killed."

Mrs. Peacock sipped her tea. "That doesn't prove anything."

"You have a paper cut on your finger. Paper cuts happen when you're in a hurry with papers, and scoop them all together. You snatched all the papers off the dining room table after you killed John. John had collected them, and showed them to you. They prove you killed Sir Hugh. He would have made sure you went to jail for that."

Mrs. Peacock laughed. "That's it? You base your accusation on a few letters written by Hugh?"

"Oh, no. I have much more evidence. You all told me different accounts of what happened the day Sir Hugh died. It was early morning, it was nearly noon. It was a fine day, it was a cold day, it was raining. Colonel Mustard was at the top of the waterfall path, or he was at the bottom beside the pool. Someone saw Sir Hugh in the water, and another person didn't. Mother packed a picnic for two, but Mrs. White made lunch for all. So I disregarded all that and paid attention to what I know best–

shoes. Mrs. White and Colonel Mustard both said Mother was dressed for the weather in Wellingtons. Mother said she stopped on the path to tie her shoelaces. Wellingtons don't have shoelaces. Sir Hugh was seen in Italian walking shoes or hip waders. If he had his walking stick, he wouldn't be wearing hip waders."

No one interrupted her, so she carried on. This was a wonderfully attentive audience. "Mrs. White says Sir Hugh was angry about being asked to change his will. After he left, Mother followed him. She pushed him over the cliff. Probably hit him with her umbrella first. Colonel Mustard didn't go fishing at all. He probably went to the shops for something to eat before lunch. He just made up his story." She swept her arms out wide. "And that is the whole truth of it."

She stopped. There was no applause. Mrs. White glared at Colonel Mustard. Everyone else glared at Mrs. Peacock. Miss Scarlet sighed. It would be hard to cajole anyone into helping her write pool party invitations now.

OLD
MONEY

The dining room glowed in gilt, silver and mahogany under the muted lights of the chandeliers. Another evening of fine dining, or at least dining in fine surroundings. The damask tablecloth was set to perfection. Too bad the dinner wouldn't be cooked the same. Mrs. Peacock snapped her linen napkin, picked up the pearl-handled fish knife and studied the insignia. "Excuse me, Mrs. White, but are these family heirlooms?"

Mrs. White paused on her way back to the kitchen. "No, they're from the fishmonger. He gives out a free knife for every pound of plaice bought. I've such a set of them now."

Mrs. Peacock replaced the knife and studied the rest of the setting with a critical eye. Two knives, three forks, three spoons, four plates. What was the real thing, and what was puffed-up fakery? One could gauge a young man's potential as a son-in-law by the value of his tableware.

The plates were trimmed in gold. The pattern was an old one, Royal Worcester from 1850, and worn off in places. These plates had been bought by Sir Hugh's mother or grandmother. She rolled over one of the regular forks. Sterling silver, heavy, elegant, also fairly old, as the tips of the tines were thin with use. Purchased with old money. John Boddy had not thought fit to update the table service in the twelve years since Hugh had died and he'd inherited the mansion. Not that a young man of eighteen attending college would put tableware at the top of his Must Be Purchased list. But after he graduated and returned to live here in 1918, with the Great War over, surely then he'd turn his attention to the finer things. She lifted the hem of the tablecloth. How old was this?

"Penny for your thoughts, Mother?"

Mrs. Peacock glanced up. Her daughter was bedecked in evening wear, white shoulders and slinky vermilion gown. A little over-the-top for dinner at Tudor Hall. "Just considering John Boddy's net worth as a suitor."

"For you? Mother, you can't be serious! He's half your age and you've been married three times!"

"No, not for me, Josephine, for you. Please keep your voice down." She dropped the tablecloth hem and it swung back into place. Top quality damask. At least forty years old.

"Oh." Miss Scarlet sank into her seat. "It's hard to keep your voice down and carry on a conversation in here. The chairs are so far apart."

"Three sword lengths, the Colonel says. Mrs. White no doubt sees this as a way to set six places on a twenty-foot table and have the overall effect look balanced."

Miss Scarlet stood and minced her way around the table. Clearly her shoes were too tight.

"John Boddy is my age and quite a dish. But is he a good prospect? Are you trying to marry me off before I become a rich and famous actress?"

"I'm trying to marry you off before you bleed me dry. I can see the Black family has had money in the past." She indicated the tableware. "I'm trying to see if Mr. Boddy has money, or just living on an allowance."

"Of course he's living on an allowance, Mother, until his birthday in two weeks. Then he inherits everything. That's why we're here."

"Yes, but the question is, how much is there to inherit? Is there enough capital to keep a mansion like this functioning? Is there money to spare for trips abroad or lavish parties? It doesn't do to marry a man whose wealth is all tied up in maintenance costs. There's no fun to be had."

Miss Scarlet clasped her hands in a gesture intended to look thoughtful, but which only looked apologetic. "So you think I shouldn't set my cap for him until we have worked this out."

"I think it would be hasty. Especially since you are the only eligible young lady here at present, and could turn his head if you chose. We must consider first the tableware. Why has he not replaced this aging china? Either, as a bachelor, he's just not interested in appearances. Or he likes the old sets. Or he's no money to spare to buy new tableware."

"Or he's waiting until he marries so his bride can choose."

"Quite. So we must search for something he has purchased in the last twelve years and see if he's bought quality or not."

"You mean posh or cheap." Miss Scarlet giggled.

"If you wish to be vulgar about it, yes."

"This sounds like a lark. A scavenger hunt for pricey or paltry."

"Hush, here are the others coming for dinner. We must be discreet." Mrs. Peacock dabbed at the corner of her mouth with her linen napkin, and smiled toward the door.

Miss Scarlet swiveled her way back to her seat under the noses of the four men entering the dining room. Colonel Mustard cleared his throat. Professor Plum's Adam's apple bobbed violently and his bow tie twitched. Mr. Green's eyes locked on her earrings like a jeweler assessing diamonds. John Boddy paid no attention at all. His interest was focused in some papers, which he hastily stuffed in his pocket when he reached his chair.

They were barely settled when Mrs. White entered with a large tray. "Here, then, I've created a treat for the first course. Pâté de foie gras.

Some foreign dish, I think. I read about it in the *Daily Mirror*. I only had to make one or two substitutions. Who has time to mess about with puff pastry? I thought a couple of slices of white bread would be easier." She placed small plates in front of each of them and returned to the kitchen.

Colonel Mustard stroked his moustache. "This doesn't look quite the ticket for pâté. What do you think, Mrs. Peacock?"

"I think it appears to be boiled plaice rolled up in bread and sprinkled with lemon and a sprig of parsley." She took a tiny bite. "Bland, but not objectionable. However, a long way from the pâté I've had in Paris."

"We can tuck in safely, then." Colonel Mustard picked up his fish knife and fork and sliced off a mouthful. "Bland to the point of nearly tasteless, I should say." He raised an eyebrow at Mr. Boddy. "When you inherit the house, you inherit the staff, I expect. A rum deal, Boddy."

John Boddy just shrugged and smoothed the pocket of papers.

Ten minutes later Mrs. White whirled in with the main course. "I've worked all day on this. Tighnabruaich rabbit stew, with onions and carrots. Mashed potatoes on the side. I didn't happen to have a fresh rabbit, so I substituted boiled sheep's tongues; there were a few of them in the pantry." She worked her way around the table with the large serving dishes, spooning the meal onto their dinner plates. When she finished, she left the dishes at the foot of the table and returned to the kitchen.

Professor Plum sighed. "Boiled tongue. Mum Plum used to make that in hard times after Papa Plum disappeared. I never did like it."

"An acquired taste, my boy," Colonel Mustard said. "Never acquired the taste myself. More potatoes, anyone?" He reached for the large bowl of fluffy white mashed potatoes and scooped himself a quantity.

Mrs. Peacock poked her way around the bits of tongue and ate the carrots. Mrs. White was clearly not up to standard as a cook. She could understand John Boddy keeping her on after years of faithful service to Sir Hugh. Why didn't he promote her out of the kitchen and hire a cook? Or settle a sum on her so she could retire? Had he not noticed her failings, or could he not afford to pay more staff?

She pondered this through a mercifully ordinary dessert of rice pudding with raisins. They trooped toward the lounge for after-dinner tea.

In the passageway, Miss Scarlet grabbed her elbow and pointed at the walls. "What do you think all these paintings are worth?"

"Some of them are only valuable to family, others would fetch a packet if sold. None of them are new. But if they were sold, other paintings would have to be bought to put in their place. The wallpaper is positively ruined behind them. Ask him if there are any artists he prefers, or is thinking of hanging. If he says he's found some sketches by his mother, we'll know he can't afford real art."

Miss Scarlet nodded and shimmied her way onto the arm of Mr. Boddy's chair as the men gathered around the table for a game of court whist.

With tea in hand, Mrs. Peacock wandered around the room as if bored. Her eyes darted from ornament to artifact. On the mantle she estimated the Akhenaten gray limestone bust, the Tutankhamun white alabaster face cream jar, and the Ramses II ebony black leopard were the real things, possibly provided by Professor Plum. She'd heard Sir Hugh sent him on archeological digs in Egypt after he'd left Oxford University.

There were two Picassos on one wall near the small mirror. They were ugly things, and did not match the ambiance of the room, but Mr. Boddy, not Sir Hugh, must have bought them as Picasso was the current darling of the art world in Paris. So either Mr. Boddy had bad taste, or he was investing in a new artist.

She strolled out of the lounge into the front hall. The usual hodgepodge of ancestral portraits hung there, and a seventeenth century suit of armor. The table was Louis Quatorze, if she wasn't mistaken, and a handsome piece it was. Nothing in this room had been sold to pay the bills, as there were no faded or scuffed empty spots on the walls.

On the passageway walls flanking the library, she encountered the most recent family portraiture. 1893, according to the brass plaques affixed, and the same artist, someone quite good but unknown to her. The first featured Sir Hugh Black, standing proudly before a mantel, sneering out at the world like a man who pulls too many strings and controls too many people. His black suit was tight-fitting, his tall collar crisply white, and his hands gripped a sheaf of papers as if they were accounts payable, instead of painter's props.

Next, his sister, Margaret Black, seated in a straight-backed chair, looking forlorn and angry. She was wearing a high-necked lacy frock, and her hair was tightly curled against her head. This was the year before she was married, when she was nearing thirty and considered an old maid.

Further along, close to the billiard room, a portrait of John Boddy, son of Margaret Black and Samuel Boddy. Painted in 1917, three years after Sir Hugh had died, when John had graduated from college and come back to Tudor Hall at age twenty-one as the master of all he surveyed. It was a casual portrait, John with a lopsided grin, dressed in tweeds and standing in the hall, one hand loosely in his pants pocket, one knee slightly bent. He looked like a man who'd just received a new toy and wanted to show it off. Of course, the mansion was his new toy, that's why he was painted in the front hall, welcoming everyone in to admire his booty. His shoes were freshly polished, his shirt collar starched, his ascot folded to perfection. A man with an eye to style.

Mrs. Peacock smiled. Add that to the list of Mr. Boddy's good points.

A man who dressed stylishly would want his wife to do likewise. Mr. Boddy would need deep pockets. Josephine's idea of stylish included new outfits every time she glanced at herself in a mirror. Imagine the relief of having a husband responsible for those bills, instead of a mother.

"Admiring the paintings, are we?" Mrs. White asked as she rounded the corner with another tea tray. "The young man as painted Master Boddy has gone off to seek his fortune in the art world in London."

"They are quite lovely. Both excellent artists. Sir Hugh looks especially imposing."

"As he might. His father had just died and he'd inherited the estate. He had responsibility on his shoulders. All that money to manage and a house to maintain. I was hired a year or so after that, after his sister got married to Samuel Boddy and ran off to America. My Winslow, rest his soul, was the chauffeur. Anyroad, it worked well for me, as I'm still here. Sir Hugh never bothered replacing staff who left, so I've a lot to do."

"Yes, I met Margaret and Samuel in America. He was a respected journalist and author. I expect they had some capital to build on with her share of her parents' estate."

"I heard she took a lump-sum payment and the proceeds from the sale of a summer home. Samuel managed it for her. Sir Hugh told Master Boddy, when he was heading off to college at eighteen, in the nine years of their marriage his mother's net worth doubled."

Increased wealth. Mrs. Peacock felt her heart flutter. Thank heaven for servants who listen at doors. "I suppose all that fell to John on their deaths?"

"It did. He was only a young lad of eight, so Sir Hugh took over the management of it. 'Twas all to fall to Master Boddy's hands on his twenty-first birthday. Here's him at twenty-one," Mrs. White pointed to the next portrait, "looking forward to his windfall of his mother's money. He thought it would suit him well, while he waited for Sir Hugh's will to give over. Only another two weeks to wait for that lot, and him on an allowance from Sir Hugh these last twelve years."

"He looks cheery enough."

Mrs. White shook her head. "Oh, he was right chuffed, and optimistic. Never thought for a moment there'd be any problem with his mother's money. Didn't think it would take him years to untangle Sir Hugh's doings."

A little alarm bell rang in the back of Mrs. Peacock's head. "Was there a problem with his mother's money? Did he inherit?"

"Hasn't seen a penny of it yet, he hasn't. He's been poring through papers for months. I think he may have gotten to the nub of it today. He's looking grim. Care for some more tea?"

"Yes, thank you." She held out her cup.

Mrs. White poured. "I'll carry on then. They're no doubt thirsty in the lounge, and this pot's not getting any hotter."

"Interesting Picassos in the lounge. Did Mr. Boddy choose them?"

"No, they were in lieu of money from some gentleman, to square up his dealings with Sir Hugh. Supposed to be some popular painter in Paris. Not to my taste." Mrs. White hoisted her silver tray.

Mrs. Peacock watched her leave, then turned her attention back to the portrait of John Boddy. A cheerful young man, expecting to have his monthly allowance from his uncle's estate augmented by his mother's entire fortune. No wonder he hired a portrait artist. He tottered on the edge of being well-heeled.

Miss Scarlet came swinging down the passageway. "The men are having an awful row in the lounge," she said. "John lost at cards and now he's blaming the others. He says Professor Plum was playing badly,

Colonel Mustard was cheating, and Mr. Green was palming cards. They're having a set-to. Mrs. White all but threw the pot of tea at them to calm them down. I expect we shall hear doors slamming quite soon."

"So this would not be a good time to return to the lounge?"

"No, I think we'd be better off in the conservatory, well out of earshot." Miss Scarlet cast a bored eye over the paintings. "Family portrait gallery?"

"Yes. That's Sir Hugh and this is his sister, John's mother Margaret."

"Oh, horrors," Miss Scarlet said. "Look at that suit." She pointed at the portrait of John Boddy.

"That suit is perfectly in style for the year of the painting. He looks rather dashing."

"But Mother, that's the same suit he has on today. The collar and cuffs are frayed, and someone has mended the elbow, but it's the same. Right down to the ascot, although it's faded."

Mrs. Peacock stared at the painting. "Are you sure?"

"Of course I'm sure. I've been staring at the frayed shirt collar this last half hour watching him play that interminable card game."

"Hmm. This doesn't bode well. Nine years in the same suit."

"Perhaps he doesn't like shopping. Perhaps he's waiting for a wife to shop for him."

"Perhaps he has less money than he ought to have. I'm going to go and look at him, even if they are beating each other with candlesticks by now. If his suit is as you say, we may have to reconsider your prospects."

They found the lounge nearly deserted. The playing cards were scattered. A redware clay jar lay cracked on the hearth. John Boddy was slumped over the card table, and a lead pipe lay on the carpet beside him.

Mrs. Peacock stepped to his side. "You're quite right Josephine. It is the same suit, and his shirt is frayed. Look, there are holes in the soles of his shoes." She straightened up. "I hope Mrs. White can find a better suit to bury him in. He's quite dead."

"What do we do now? Look at Professor Plum as the next best suitor, as he's not too old?"

"No, silly. We call the authorities. Boddy is dead and will have to be looked after. Go and tell Mrs. White. I've some other business to attend to."

As Miss Scarlet hurried toward the kitchen, Mrs. Peacock slipped her hand inside Mr. Boddy's pocket and extracted the papers she'd seen him tuck there at dinner. She tiptoed across the hall to the study, closed and locked the door. Mrs. White had said she thought John was looking particularly grim, as if he had found the drain where his mother's money had leaked away.

In the study, she sat down and spread the papers on the desk. Sir Hugh's accounts, cross-referenced and annotated. By the looks of it, John had cobbled together several leads to get to the hub of the financial scramble, resulting in his summary pages of neatly scripted totals.

The Expenses sheet was revealing. Standing orders for allowances to a number of people, including all the visiting gentlemen and herself. Even Miss Scarlet was listed. How dare she! Receiving money from Sir Hugh's estate in one hand and holding out her other hand begging for Mummy's cash. The next time, there would be empty hands waving back at her.

Another page showed expenses drawn against the estate of Margaret Black Boddy. Tuition at boarding school. Anthropology texts at Oxford. Field trips. For a young anthropology student, John Boddy had taken quite a few trips to Egypt. She would have thought he'd have spent more time in the classroom. Surely only graduates toddled off to the tombs of pharaohs and sent home relics.

She heard voices from the lounge. The alarm had been sounded, and the guests had gathered to decry and protest. She ought to join the commotion.

A moment later, she stood at the lounge door watching.

Mrs. White tugged at her apron. "What to become of me now? Who's to take over the house and keep me as housekeeper? Who's going to clean up this mess? I hope that clay jar wasn't worth much, as it's ruined now."

Professor Plum had an arm tentatively around Miss Scarlet's shoulders. "Actually, it was worth a lot. Egyptian, redware clay jar, 3200 BC, Late Predynastic period. I'd say there are plenty more where that came from, but there aren't, really."

Miss Scarlet whimpered into a hanky. "Oh dear, oh how sad, what is to become of me, oh woe." She touched her forehead with a limp wrist.

Right. That would be the shocked and shaken ingénue performance. Mrs. Peacock felt like applauding. Only weakly, as one does to acknowledge the performance but not encourage an encore.

Mr. Green sought his leather book between the cushions of the chintz chesterfield. "Blessed are those who break pots of clay, for they shall earn vessels of gold." He picked up a porcelain figurine of a Victorian lady in his damp pudgy fingers. "I shall take care of this, lest it get broken in the impending confusion." He slid the figurine into his pea green jacket pocket.

"Order. Order, please. Please vacate the room. That is an order." Colonel Mustard tapped his riding crop on the mantel, knocking down an Egyptian terracotta dish, which shattered on the tiled hearth.

Mrs. White gasped. So did Professor Plum.

Mrs. Peacock felt enough was enough. She spoke up. "I accuse you of killing Mr. Boddy in the lounge with the lead pipe."

OLD MONEY

SOLUTION:

Consternation rippled through the room as they all stared accusingly at each other.

"I mean you, Professor Plum."

Professor Plum frowned. "Why would I do that?"

"John Boddy threatened to cut off your allowance from Sir Hugh."

"He threatened to cut off Colonel Mustard's and Mr. Green's too. He was angry about the card game. He'd have changed his mind by morning."

"He threatened to stop paying for your summer archeological digs."

"There are other sources of funding. The British Museum, for example."

"Mr. Boddy had discovered his mother's money was spent to pay for your education and summer jaunts. You know the value of these broken artifacts because you dug them up in Egypt. You said yourself you and your mother had fallen on hard times after your father's disappearance. Sir Hugh used his sister's money to pay your way. Boddy asked for it back. Demanded it back. You couldn't pay. He probably threatened to take you to court. So you killed him to protect yourself from bankruptcy and disgrace."

Professor Plum hung his head. "A man can only risk so much."

Mrs. Peacock shrugged. "You've traded bankruptcy and disgrace for jail. I fear you've come out on the deficit side."

Miss Scarlet sniffed and moved away from his sheltering arm. "I have quite run out of potential suitors here."

A DESIGNATED CASUALTY

The rain tippled down, rushing in noisy channels along the downspouts. Through the streaked windows, the sky was ominously gray.

Professor Plum settled into the green leather chair in the lounge with the morning paper open at the crossword puzzle. He'd have to work slowly to make this puzzle fill the day. The others seemed gainfully employed. John Boddy was in his study, reading the morning's post. The rest were here in the lounge. Colonel Mustard was snoring with an atlas on his lap. Mr. Green was examining the family treasures in the curio cabinet and fiddling with the lock. Mrs. Peacock seemed engrossed in her book. Presumably Mrs. White slaved in the kitchen over a pot of coffee and a mound of shortbread. Or treacle scones. Or currant buns. His mouth watered just thinking about such delights. Especially after the grotesque breakfast of cold chopped sardines on dry toast.

The door opened with a creak of ancient hinges. Miss Scarlet dragged herself into the room wearing a trailing fluffy pink silky thing that didn't look like day wear.

"Is there any coffee? I'm desperate for coffee." She flung a hand to her forehead like a melodramatic heroine. "Oh look, it's raining. How depressing. What will we do today if it's raining?"

Colonel Mustard roused himself and looked at her with disapproval.

Mr. Green turned his back to the curio cabinets and gazed at the ceiling like a child in a sweet shop pretending he hasn't pinched anything.

Mrs. Peacock glanced over the top of her book. "If you'd gotten up for breakfast, Josephine, you'd have noticed the rain hours ago. That nice young postman was absolutely dripping."

"So was the letter he was holding," Professor Plum said. "Shame, as the envelope had an interesting foreign stamp. It would do for someone's collection. That's what we could do today, work on Mr. Boddy's stamp collection. I'm sure he has one. Everybody has one."

"I'll go and inquire, shall I?" Colonel Mustard stood up and strode out of the room.

"See, Josephine, you've upset the Colonel's sensibilities. He doesn't like to see young ladies parading around in nightwear." Mrs. Peacock turned a page in her book. "Mrs. White will be along with elevenses shortly. Why don't you go and get dressed instead of moping around here, waiting?"

Miss Scarlet pouted and flounced out of the room in a silky rustle.

Professor Plum stared at the spot where she had stood. Was that nightwear, that voluminous pink concoction with lace and feathers running up and down the length of it? How did women sleep with all that wrapped around them? *Concoction.* That might fit in Twelve Down. He penciled that in and paused, so as not to rush the conclusion of the crossword.

Ah, here Mrs. White was now, and the silver tray was laden with, yes, currant buns. Big fat currant buns stuffed with plump currants and dripping with butter. A man could fill his tummy with four and be carried all the way to dinner, where his rescue lay in mashed potatoes.

Colonel Mustard followed her closely, looking like a man as desperate for sustenance as the rest of them. "No stamp collection. Sorry. We'll have to make do with tiddly-winks."

Professor Plum was on his third bun and second cup of coffee when Miss Scarlet reappeared, dressed demurely in a cranberry red frock with dropped waist and matching shoes. She pounced on the coffee. He was glad he already had his second cup, as he wouldn't want to challenge her for possession of the coffee pot.

When the coffee reached her bloodstream, she smiled around the room. "What shall we do today? We can't go for a walk in the rain. We need to do something active indoors. I know, let's put on a play. I'll be the heroine. Who would like to be the villain?"

"Do you have a play in mind?" Mrs. Peacock asked, turning a page of her book in slow motion. "One needs a script or at least a plot to put on a play."

"Don't suggest Shakespeare," Mr. Green said. "I never understood all those long speeches. Blessed are plain words, for they shall be spoken."

"Something with lots of action, I'd say," Colonel Mustard said. "I've just the ticket. I'll tell you the story of the skirmish of Shahjahanpur, and we can act it out. This happens to be the 25th anniversary of our action there."

"Is there a part for a beautiful young heroine?" Miss Scarlet asked.

"Of course there is. A war story wouldn't be complete without a sweet young woman, or what's the fighting for, eh?" Colonel Mustard chuckled and gave her a wink.

Professor Plum could think of several skirmishes, indeed entire battles, which did not feature heroines, but he kept his counsel. He was perilously near finishing this puzzle and hours to go before the afternoon papers arrived. "I think that's a jolly idea, putting on a play with a battle theme. Should we do it in here, or in the ballroom?"

Colonel Mustard stood up and straightened his uniform. "In the ballroom, of course. We need lots of space. I won this medal for the skirmish of Shahjahanpur." He pointed to a beribboned gold medal on his chest inscribed with some Latin words and imprinted with a crest. "So you can bet it was a dramatic fight. I'll fetch some props while you finish your coffee. Shall we say, fifteen minutes? Tally-ho."

Miss Scarlet gave the coffee her full attention for the next fifteen minutes. "All right, people, places!" She smiled. "That's what they say on movie sets in Hollywood. Come along then, everyone. To the ballroom with you."

She ushered them into the passageway and ducked her head into the study. "That means you, too, John Boddy. Come on, leave those boring old papers. This will only take ten minutes."

Professor Plum did not believe that. It took an hour for Colonel Mustard to tell a story. It would take longer to perform it. He saw Mr. Boddy tuck his papers in his inner pocket as he followed Miss Scarlet down the passageway.

The gray skies dulled the gilt frames of the ancestral portraits in the ballroom. Even the wall sconce at the top of the curved staircase couldn't disperse the gloom. Colonel Mustard came in carrying six revolvers, with a seventh tucked in his belt. "Here, I've taken the liberty of borrowing some of Sir Hugh's gun collection. I've loaded them all with blanks. They're quite safe at a distance of more than ten feet, and they make an authentic racket." He laid the six guns on the lid of the grand piano.

"Blanks? Where did you get blanks?" Mr. Green picked up the first gun and turned it over in his pudgy hands.

"Every landowner has blanks. One uses blanks to train horses not to shy away from gunfire."

"Sir Hugh bought a few boxes of blanks when Queen Victoria died, for the twenty-one-gun salute in the village," Mrs. White said. "That was quite a day. People came from all over the countryside. We had a fête on the lawn, it was ever so nice."

"Quite. If we could return to the task at hand. If you'll all choose a gun."

"I've used one of these before," Miss Scarlet said. "We shot blanks in one theatre production I was in, *The Hatfields and the McCoys*."

"I say, could you give us a demonstration?" Professor Plum asked. "It seems rash to go running around the ballroom with real revolvers."

"My pleasure." Colonel Mustard took one of the guns from the piano and aimed it at a gold brocade chair about twelve feet away. "Remember, I am an excellent marksman." He pulled the trigger. The gun exploded with a loud bang, and nothing happened to the chair. Instead, a flurry of grey dust settled on the floor near the gun's muzzle. "Satisfied?"

"Yes," Professor Plum said. "I'll take that one, please." He took the gun and held it at arm's length. It was warm.

"I'm sure I don't know what I'm doing here, with dishes to wash and lunch to make," Mrs. White said. "I'll be off, then."

"No, indeed, we need you," Colonel Mustard said, placing a revolver in her hand. "We need everyone. You can play the part of a rebel. Perhaps we should begin by setting the scene. It was a narrow street in Shahjahanpur. My scouting party and I were seeking a safe route through the town for the artillery, when we were set upon by rebels."

"So where's the narrow street?" Professor Plum asked.

"We'll make one," Miss Scarlet said, selecting a gun from the piano. "Move that potted palm over beside the grand piano, and Mr. Green, you can move the gold brocade chairs into a line facing the piano. That gives us a marked straight corridor from the piano to the grand staircase. How does that look, Colonel?"

"Excellent, Miss Scarlet. Picture this, if you will. A narrow cobbled street leading from the hills to the center of the village. On the left and right are houses and shops. There are people going about their business. You, Miss Scarlet, stand here."

Colonel Mustard directed her to a spot to the left of the base newel post of the grand staircase.

"Am I the heroine?"

"Yes, you are the lovely young shopkeeper of the café. When the skirmish starts, you step out of your establishment to see what the commotion is all about. Mrs. White and Mrs. Peacock, you take positions here on the steps as the rebel forces."

"I'll not be running up and down the steps, if that's what you're thinking," Mrs. White said. "My old knees won't stand for it."

"There'll be no running. Your mission is to shoot at the advancing soldiers."

"Is that the commotion you spoke about?" Mrs. Peacock asked. "Soldiers and rebels shooting?"

"Yes, it is."

"Then that shopkeeper would be a foolish person indeed to step out into the street with shooting going on." Mrs. Peacock sat down on the staircase and flicked a feather from her hat out of her face.

"Nevertheless, that's what she did, and we can't change the course of history just to suit our more refined sensibilities."

"Hmm. My daughter is well-cast, then, as the girl with no brains."

"Mother!"

"Can we get on with it?" Mrs. White asked. "I've potatoes to peel and all."

"Quite so. Now then, Green, Boddy and Plum, you shall take the parts of my soldiers. We are advancing up the street, seeking a safe route for the artillery. We're not expecting any resistance. We didn't know about the forty rebels."

"Aye, aye, Colonel." Mr. Green wiped a speck of dust from his immaculate jade suit lapel.

"I was only a Captain then, with ten men in my advance party."

"Aye, aye, Captain." Mr. Green straightened his lime silk tie. "Professor Plum, Mr. Boddy and I are acting the part of ten men, are we? Blessed are the multiplied. That calls for some scurrying. And we're to walk from the end of the chairs here to the top of the stairs, shooting?"

"You'll not take the top of the stairs without going through me," Mrs. White said.

"Indeed he shan't," Colonel Mustard said. "I'd tell you how the skirmish turned out, but that would spoil the drama. Instead, I'll whisper secret instructions to each of you."

"Oh, goody, I love secrets." Miss Scarlet clapped her hands. "Who can I tell mine to?"

"Josephine, the essence of a secret is that it not be told." Mrs. Peacock frowned. "Is this how you've treated all my secrets over the years? Sought out the first available set of ears and blabbered?"

"Where's the fun in not telling?" Miss Scarlet pouted. "You can't make a conversation out of not talking."

"It'll be finished raining by the time we start at this rate," Mr. Green said. "What next, Captain?"

Colonel Mustard stroked his moustache. "Let me place each one of you. Green, Boddy and Plum, side by side at the potted plant. You'll be advancing toward the stairs. Ladies, half-way up the stairs crouching against the banisters. You'll be coming down the stairs, somewhat furtively as you are the rebels, with no discernible leadership. Miss Scarlet, stand at the base of the staircase, as if you are in your shop. When we start shooting, you are to come out and inquire."

"Inquire? I think I'd be screaming blue murder." Mrs. White smoothed her apron.

"That's hardly fair odds, four of you against Mrs. White and me," Mrs. Peacock said. "Especially when we're taking the part of forty rebels. We want John Boddy on our side."

"Right enough." Mrs. White nodded. "Master Boddy ought to be a rebel, then it's three against three."

"Very well, then. Boddy, if you would oblige and join the ladies up the staircase."

John Boddy shrugged and climbed the stairs.

"If the rebels are coming down from the hills and the scouting party is advancing up the street toward the hills, how is anyone going to get to the center of town?" Professor Plum scratched his head. "It seems to me the scouting party is just leaving town, walking right into the rebels' stronghold."

Colonel Mustard exhaled and his face flushed. "We didn't know about the rebels. And the streets were a bit of a maze, not laid out neatly like ours. We thought we were heading to the center of town. Please, just try to follow my orders."

"Orders? I'm still waiting for my secret instructions," Mrs. White said. "I think I'll sit down."

"I don't think the streets of London are laid out neatly," Professor Plum said.

"Excellent example. Imagine then, that the streets of this village are laid out much as London's are, with happenstance being key."

"Didn't you have a map?" Mrs. White asked. "What kind of scouting party goes out without a map?"

"There were no maps available. Try to concentrate on the event. Now that you're in place, I shall whisper your secret instructions." The colonel walked up the stairs and whispered something to Mrs. Peacock. She nodded.

"Could you whisper louder, Colonel?" Miss Scarlet asked. "I didn't catch that and Mother isn't about to tell me."

"No, I cannot. Hold your position. And hold your peace." Colonel Mustard glowered at her.

She sniffed and leaned on the newel post, striking poses suitable for photographs.

Slowly, Colonel Mustard made his way around the group, whispering instructions.

When he got to Professor Plum, he whispered, "You're a designated casualty. You're advancing on the street, looking for a clear wide passage for the artillery. When the rebels start shooting, shoot back for a few minutes and then fall down dead, as if you'd been shot."

Professor Plum nodded. This was going to be jolly fun. Perhaps Miss Scarlet would run around administering first aid. Or checking for vital signs. He'd groan a bit before he 'died' for good effect.

"Does everyone understand their orders?" Colonel Mustard looked at them. They all nodded. "Let's begin then." He stepped to the center of the 'street' and snapped to attention, his back to the staircase. "Company, fall in!"

Mr. Green looked at Professor Plum. Professor Plum looked at Mr. Green.

"Are we to commence with the secret instructions or are we to follow this new order?" Mr. Green asked. "Blessed are the succinct, for they shall be heeded."

"The secret instructions are for the climax. We're just starting the action." Colonel Mustard whacked his riding crop against his pant leg. "Can you people not follow a simple plan?"

"I didn't get any secret instructions," Miss Scarlet said, pouting.

"You don't need secret instructions. I told you what you were to do."

"But everyone else got a secret and I didn't. That's not fair."

"If the Colonel gave you a secret, you'd tell someone before we started the play." Mrs. Peacock stretched her legs. "Perhaps you'll be the one involved in the surprise ending."

Colonel Mustard sighed, walked over to Miss Scarlet, and whispered something in her ear.

"Really?" she said, her eyes bright. "Well, let's get started. Lights, Camera, Action!"

"I don't think there was a camera, Miss Scarlet," Professor Plum pointed out. "It was Shahjahanpur, you'll remember. Not the kind of place you'd take a camera to, I'm sure."

"Professor, that's Hollywood talk for Let's Get Started." Miss Scarlet rolled her eyes as if she had never met a more illiterate person.

"Oh. I see. Carry on, then."

Colonel Mustard drew himself to attention again. "Company, fall in!"

Mr. Green and Professor Plum lined up in front of him.

"Stand at attention!" Colonel Mustard bellowed. "What kind of soldiers fall in with sloppy posture?"

"Civilian soldiers?" Professor Plum guessed.

"Never mind." Colonel Mustard pressed two fingers against the bridge of his nose. After a moment, he straightened up and resumed his authoritative voice. "Company, our mission is to scout out a clear path through this town which follows us for the artillery. Keep alert. Forward March!"

He swiveled on his heels and began marching in tiny steps toward the staircase, his neck snapping this way and that as if looking for lurkers in the line of chairs. As they moved along, he nodded to Mrs. Peacock. She stood up.

Mrs. White stood up beside her. Mr. Boddy leaned on the banister.

Colonel Mustard held up a hand. "Could I have some more enthusiasm, ladies? This is a skirmish, not a recital. Start shooting."

"Might I remind you I only have six 'bullets'," Mrs. Peacock said, holding out her gun. "If I use them all in the first minute, I'll be helpless."

"Everyone will discharge their weapons at the same rate. You'll all be out of ammunition at the same time. Then our play will be over. Look lively. Let's do that again. All together."

"Before we do, were they shooting at us?" Professor Plum asked. "Because if they are, ought we to shoot back?"

"Of course you shoot back," Colonel Mustard shouted. "You're a soldier."

"Not really. I'm a professor."

"Today you're an actor," Miss Scarlet said. "Throw you heart into it. Give it some gumption." She waved her hands in the air. "Be the best soldier ever! Save the world!"

Colonel Mustard turned to the staircase. "If we could do that bit again, Mrs. Peacock."

Once again Colonel Mustard started marching toward the staircase. Mr. Green and Professor Plum followed.

Mrs. Peacock, Mrs. White, and Mr. Boddy began shooting. Mr. Green and Professor Plum shot back. The sound of gunfire ricocheted off the high ornate plaster ceilings. The air turned blue with the dust from the disintegrating blanks.

Colonel Mustard glanced over his shoulder, his eyes glinting. "Careful, men! The rebels have come down from the hills," he shouted. "Take cover. Watch for civilians. Shoot the rebels." He waved his riding crop in the air.

Miss Scarlet stepped out from her place beside the newel post. "Hold your fire while I say my lines. Here I go." She struck a dramatic heroine pose. "What's going on? What's all the noise?" she shouted, waving her arms and spinning around. "Hark, is that the rebel force come down from the hills to protect our village from the advancing army? Who will save me from certain death? Help, oh help!"

"I'll save you, Miss," Colonel Mustard cried. He stepped in front of her and shielded her body from both sets of guns. "You'll not harm this lady while I am Captain of this expedition. Shoot, men, shoot them all!" He brandished his riding crop with one hand and pulled his gun from his belt with the other. He started shooting.

The others began shooting again, too. Mrs. White sat down on the staircase and flopped back to lean against the stairs. Behind her, Boddy, cast himself backwards with arms outstretched. On the 'street', Mr. Green fell over lightly and propped himself up on one elbow.

Professor Plum fired twice more, and found he was out of ammunition. He sank to the floor and groaned as loudly as he could. For good measure, he twitched a little before lying still. He'd seen that in the cowboy moving pictures. He kept his eyes open in little slits, so he could watch the rest of the show.

In the ensuing lack of gunfire, Mrs. Peacock slumped to the steps and leaned against the railings.

"Alas, my entire unit has been killed," Colonel Mustard shouted. "But we killed all the rebels! The streets are safe for the artillery advancement." He turned to Miss Scarlet. "You, lovely lady shopkeeper, are saved from an unfortunate death, caught in the crossfire of opposing forces. Next time, stay indoors when you hear shooting."

He stepped to one side and thrust her back to the newel post.

"I didn't get a chance to use my gun," Miss Scarlet complained.

Professor Plum wondered if that was the end of the performance. It was hard to tell, since there was no applause.

"That took long enough," Mrs. White said, getting up. "I've no time to cook the parsnips for lunch. You'll have to settle for boiled eggs."

"I'm sure we'll all be content with eggs, Mrs. White." Mrs. Peacock flicked a wrist. "Don't you all agree?"

"I say, I think that's a perfect lunch," Professor Plum said, getting up and straightening his bow tie.

"I enjoyed that, it was absolutely thrilling," Miss Scarlet said. "Is that how you got your medal, Colonel? For being the last man standing and saving the poor damsel in distress?"

"This medal, and a promotion up from Captain, yes." Colonel Mustard gave the gold medal a quick buff with his sleeve. "One of my proudest moments."

"And it's stopped raining," Mr. Green said, standing up and brushing his pant legs. "I think I'll take a stroll around the grounds, refresh my thoughts."

Mrs. Peacock smoothed her skirt. "You can get up now, John. The show's over. John?"

Mrs. White stepped closer to him. "Master Boddy? Are you all right? Twist your ankle in the fall?"

Mrs. Peacock leaned over him. "Worse than that. I think he's dead. He's been shot." She looked down at the gun in her hand.

Professor Plum swallowed. It was like being inside an oil painting. All the people standing frozen, holding guns, with one inert form as the focus of attention. He swallowed again. Had he done this, with his revolver shooting blanks? Could you kill someone with blanks? He was sure he was more than ten feet from the staircase.

Breaking through his inertia, he hurried forward to press a hand to Mr. Boddy's chest, seeking a heartbeat. He found none. However, he did find a letter peeking out of Mr. Boddy's inner breast pocket. He slid it out and glanced over it while he pretended to take a pulse.

Ah-ha. He turned to face the waiting group. "Indeed, Mrs. Peacock is right. Mr. Boddy has been shot. I accuse you of killing Mr. Boddy in the ballroom with the revolver." He pointed his revolver at the assumed guilty party.

A
DESIGNATED
CASUALTY

SOLUTION:

"My dear boy. I'm a soldier. I don't go around shooting civilians." Colonel Mustard tapped his riding crop on the hardwood floor for emphasis.

"You loaded the revolvers. You put blanks in all but one, and placed them on the piano for our use. You kept the live-ammunition one for yourself, tucked in your belt." Professor Plum pointed to Colonel Mustard's belt. "In the process of saving the damsel in distress, you didn't do as much shooting as the rest of us. You possibly only shot once or twice. Certainly you didn't shoot after Boddy went down."

"And you took note of all that, did you? In the heat of the battle?"

"My gun was tested at the chair before we began. I know that I had five shots, and I aimed at all three people on the stairs. Neither of the ladies fell down dead. The ladies were aiming at us, so they didn't shoot Boddy. Mr. Green, who did you aim at?"

"I aimed at the wall sconce at the top of the staircase," Mr. Green said. "It seemed an easier target, as it wasn't moving." He looked up at the shining prisms. "None of it broke so I'm sure my bullets were blanks."

Colonel Mustard harrumphed. "It's all very well to blame me, but why would I kill Boddy?"

"I think the answer is here in the letter Boddy received in this morning's post. You learned of the letter when you went to see if Mr. Boddy had a stamp collection. Let's do the reenactment again. Only this time, Miss Scarlet, I'd like you to take the role of Colonel Mustard, and the part of the shopkeeper damsel in distress will be played by the newel post. Colonel, you'll have to be the audience. Sit over there. Miss Scarlet, come and read this passage in the letter I found in Boddy's pocket. You can ad lib your lines from that, I assume."

Miss Scarlet took the letter and read it over. "I think I can manage."

"We'll not be using real guns this time, will we?" Mrs. White asked, putting her gun on the stair beside Boddy.

"We'll use our fingers, like little boys in America do when they're playing at Cowboys and Indians." Mr. Green lifted his hand with pudgy index finger pointing, thumb erect and other fingers curled in to his palm. He flicked his thumb toward his index finger twice. "Bang, bang."

They all took their places, except for Boddy who was still in his. Colonel Mustard sat frowning and tapping his riding crop in one of the chairs that formed the street.

Miss Scarlet strode to the front of the line of soldiers. "Lights, camera, action!" she shouted. "Men, storm the village! Take no prisoners!"

"Here, here," Colonel Mustard protested. "I never said that."

"No, but it sounds more dramatic than 'Company, fall in,' don't you think?"

"Could you stick to the script, please, Miss Scarlet?" Professor Plum asked. "We're trying to prove a point here."

"Oh, all right." Her shoulders flopped and she rolled her eyes to the ceiling. "Company, fall in." Her voice was totally void of enthusiasm.

They all took their places and fired the first round of imaginary shots, with vocal accompaniment. "Bang, bang, boom, bang, bang!"

They paused. Miss Scarlet began her lines. "Oh, look, rebel forces coming down from the hills to shoot us. I must take cover. Here's a little shop." She stepped closer to the newel post. "Good morning, dear lady, do you have any sweets for sale? Perhaps a currant bun or a treacle scone? Oh, I suspect you don't speak English. "Let me point. I'd like one of those, and I'll pay you with this money. Thank you."

Miss Scarlet turned to the waiting soldiers. "That's your cue to keep shooting," she said in a stage whisper.

The others commenced shooting. "Bang, bang, bang, bang." They each fell over dead as before. Professor Plum didn't bother to groan this time.

"My, that was delicious," Miss Scarlet said. "Oh, it seems like the shooting has stopped. I must be on my way. Thank you. Cheerio."

She stepped away from the newel post. "Hark, I see our artillery coming down the street. I am saved. My ten men are all dead. The rebels are all dead. I'd better empty my gun." She held up her fingers. "Bang, bang, bang, bang, bang, bang, was that six?"

Mrs. Peacock sat up and clapped once or twice. "Well done, Josephine. I can see why you are currently experiencing a stellar career as an actress. Nevertheless, if those are the facts contained in the letter, Colonel Mustard, you are the villain of the piece."

"Agreed," Professor Plum said. "So you see, the Colonel didn't receive his medal by valiant effort. He took it under false pretenses. Boddy received this letter in the morning post. It's from a villager, commenting on the 25th anniversary of the skirmish, and thanking Sir Hugh for leading the artillery up the street to liberate the town. She says the captain of the scouting party spent the skirmish inside her shop. He ran out when everyone else was dead and the artillery was rounding the corner. After receiving this letter this morning, Boddy would have turned him in. Colonel Mustard would have had to give back the medal."

"And in so doing become the laughing stock of his fellows," Mrs. Peacock added. "Well done, Professor Plum. We should give you a medal. I do think you ought to be rewarded for your astute thinking."

"There aren't any spare medals lying about," Mrs. White said. "What do you say to a reward of a special plate of herrings in oatmeal?"

BIRDS
OF A
FEATHER

Mrs. Peacock slipped down the hall on silent leather pumps. The voice was coming from the conservatory, she was sure. It was a familiar voice, yet not quite.

"Awk. Colonel Mustard, utter bore. Awk."

There it was again, her daughter Josephine's voice, but a little throatier.

"Awk. Suppose you'll be wanting tea? Awk."

No, now it sounded like Mrs. White, only more soprano in timbre. If she was speaking to Josephine, there would be a 'request for coffee' response.

"Do you have any idea how much that's worth? Awk."

That was definitely John Boddy. They must be gathered around the conservatory fountain, enjoying the sunshine and the scent of flowers. No doubt Josephine would be trying to worm her way into John's favor and thus into his inheritance. Mrs. White was attempting to interrupt the proceedings with an offer of tea.

"Awk. Mother is so stingy. Pockets of money. She won't share."

Josephine again, complaining to their host that her mother was rich and wouldn't dole out. If she only knew how close Mummy was to the end of Sir Matthew Peacock's fortune.

"Awk. Tally ho, stand down, old boy." Colonel Mustard's voice, issuing orders as usual.

She paused at the conservatory door, a hand on the doorknob. Should she wait to hear what else her ungrateful daughter said about her? No, she could guess the complaints. Mother won't give me pocket money. Mother won't buy me new shoes. Why bore Mr. Boddy with that nonsense? Prospective suitors don't hang on a young lady's every word, if all the words are whining. Mummy would be most relieved if John Boddy married Josephine. Mummy ought to prevent Josephine from spoiling her chances.

She swung the door open and adjusted her hat to keep the bright sun from her eyes.

There was no one in the room. The chairs and tables were empty. The calico ryukin fish swam in erratic ovals in the large fish tank. The fan tails lurked at the bottom near the sand, cringing under the eaves of the china castle. The aspidistra leaves showed strange green splotches while the geraniums and ivy quivered in the non-existent breeze.

Mrs. Peacock stood still and listened. She heard nothing but the rustle of the feathers on her hat. They sounded alive. It made her skin crawl.

She shook her head to whisk away the hollowness of the sound. The rustle collected into a bunch and relocated at the top of the Bismarck palm. She clamped a hand to her mouth to suppress a scream.

At the top of the Bismarck palm sat an enormous blue-green bird, eyeing her through giant black eyes. Blue-green hardly described it. Together the feathers rippled in a luxurious iridescent sheen. Individually, she could see feathers of lapis lazuli, ultramarine, aquamarine, chartreuse, jade, amethyst and heliotrope. The wing feathers were tipped with magenta. The tail was bright red. She had never seen such marvelous plumage. She circled the fountain to get a closer look.

"Blue feathers, blue feathers," the bird screamed at her and dive-bombed her hat. "Kill the bird. Blue feathers. Lots of money." Talons snatched at her skull and tore away her hat.

The bird flapped to a branch on the weeping fig tree clutching its trophy. One lonely teal feather snapped off her hat and floated down in a mesmerizing series of arcs.

Incapable of movement, Mrs. Peacock followed its progress all the way to the floor, where it settled ever so gently on the forehead of John Boddy.

Mr. Boddy lay on the tiled floor with a giant birdcage tilted on his chest and a narrow but effective crease across his skull. He had clearly gone to the Great Bird Sanctuary in the Sky.

Shaking herself free of her temporary catatonic state, Mrs. Peacock tiptoed closer.

Mr. Boddy's fingers were tangled in the wires of the cage which encumbered him. His fingers were stained an odd indigo-violet shade. Bird seed spilled out of the crystal cup and dribbled across his Harris Tweed jacket. A great slimy green glob oozed off his right shoulder and dripped on the floor.

Mrs. Peacock looked up at the bird, staring down at her over its hooked black beak. "What did you do to John Boddy?" she asked it.

"Awk. Pay me now. Valuable. Blue feathers. Wretched beast. Whack. Arrgghh." The bird tipped its head back and made a gargling sound.

Mrs. Peacock looked from the bird to the body and back. One thing was certain, she had to get her hands on some of those feathers. Her milliner would be able to make the most delightful hat. "Here, birdie, birdie, nice birdie. Come and let Mummy pluck your feathers, there's a dear."

"Awk. Mother is a cheapskate."

Mrs. Peacock glared at the bird. She shook Mr. Boddy's smudged fingers free, up-righted the two-foot square bird cage, and carried it to a wide flat space on the front edge of the fountain. "Birdie come and have a rest. Nice cagey for birdie."

The bird swooped down and plucked the handkerchief from Mr. Boddy's breast pocket. A bit of paper followed the handkerchief and slid to the floor. The bird fluttered to the door of the cage, eyeballed the interior, dropped the handkerchief, and flapped away, to the edge of the fish tank. Its brilliant red tail drooped in the water. The fish cowered.

"What's the matter with the cage? Not comfy enough?" She peered at the cage's interior. A horseshoe-shaped hoop swung near a cluster of colored toys. Something was missing. Ah, there ought to be a bar at the bottom of the horseshoe. "Birdie's lost his perch. We can't have that. Birdie needs a place to sit so Mummy can pluck him."

She glanced around the room. Why would the bird have taken its perch out of the cage? What would it look like? A cylindrical bar of some type, no doubt, with claw marks from those gunmetal gray talons. Where would it have taken the perch? To the top of one of the plants, and then dropped it. She poked around in the foliage until she spotted a lead pipe in the soil of the split-leaf philodendron. It was a little sticky, so she rinsed it in the fish tank. The fish darted madly in all directions.

The lead pipe fit neatly into the wire hoop. She stepped back to give the bird flying room. The bird did not swoop into the cage with gratitude. Why not? There was no food in the cage. Did birds eat fish? If she scooped a fresh one from the tank and tossed it in the cage, would the bird return home for a fresh feast?

There were limits to the lengths one could go in order to obtain unique feathers. Nabbing a fish with one's bare hands was beyond acceptable.

She sat down on the chaise longue to consider her options. The bird hopped and fluttered to the top of the weeping fig tree. The patter of sensible shoes arrived behind her, along with a slam of the door.

"This door needs to be kept shut as long as that bird is out of its cage." Mrs. White waved a dust cloth in the air. "Come now, bird, get back where you belong."

"I quite agree. He shouldn't be wandering at will in the ornamental plants. I've been trying to entice him into the cage," Mrs. Peacock said. "Where did this bird come from, Mrs. White?"

"He was delivered yesterday while you lot were off touring Winchester Cathedral. Master Boddy let him loose in his study, flapping around, but I said he'd be a sight better off in the conservatory, where there's no rug. He'd a devil of a time getting the wretched thing cornered, I can tell you. 'Twere no end of trouble, and that creature swooping from room to room, stealing hankies and leaving a trail of splatter."

The door opened. Mr. Green wandered in with his leather Bible in his pudgy hands. "It's a pleasant day to sit in here," he said over his shoulder. "If Professor Plum finds us a card table and Colonel Mustard brings the cards, we can have an enjoyable round of Court Whist before tea. Blessed are they that play games, for they shall be winners. Does that suit you, Miss Scarlet?"

"I suppose it's more entertaining than watching the professor work a crossword puzzle. What's that big cagey thing?"

"What the devil?" Colonel Mustard sputtered.

"Oh, I say," Professor Plum said, pulling his magnifying glass from his pocket.

Mrs. White slammed the door shut.

"Where's the bird?" Mr. Green asked, looking up, and holding his leather Bible protectively over the shoulder of his lime green suit. "You haven't lost it, have you?"

"It's up there," Mrs. White said, pointing with her cloth duster.

"Oh, I say, incredible plumage. What is it?" Professor Plum tucked his magnifying glass away.

"I don't know, but it talks." Mrs. Peacock assessed the probability of four more people being successful in repatriating the bird to its cage. Prospects were dim.

"Awk. Mother is so stingy." The bird bobbed its blue head.

Miss Scarlet flushed pink. "It's awfully pretty in a wrong-color way. It would be majestic in reds and burgundies. Does anyone know what it is?"

"This is a rare and very valuable Kamehameha Cacatua from Hawaii," Mr. Green said. "Mr. Boddy is lucky to have it. You have to get on a waiting list to receive one, and hope the birds have a successful nesting season. They're susceptible to rain, you see, and volcanic eruptions."

"Then Boddy ought to keep it in the cage," Colonel Mustard said. "Less risk of damage."

"Mr. Boddy can't do anything about it now." Mrs. Peacock got up and pointed to the body on the floor behind the fountain.

"That's a sticky wicket," Colonel Mustard said, poking the body with his riding crop. "Ought to call the authorities."

"Oh, I say. I rather think we should play Court Whist in another room." Professor Plum's bow tie wilted.

"Let's get out of here," Miss Scarlet said, yanking the door open.

The bird flapped its wings, launched off the weeping fig tree, dropped a green gooey lump on the chaise longue, and swooped out the door into the passageway, carrying Mrs. Peacock's feather hat.

Mrs. Peacock gave chase. The footsteps of the others followed her. Were they all trying to help retrieve her hat, or were they larking about, looking for excitement? The bird circled the ballroom, continued into the dining room, and came to roost in the chandelier above the dining table.

"What's it doing now, with Mother's hat and the chandelier?" Miss Scarlet asked.

"Building a nest, that's what," Mrs. White said, flapping the cloth duster at the bird. "Well, I never. He's a she, a broody hen. That's all I need, a clutch of that thieving vulture's eggs dangling above my damask. I'll get the broom."

"No, Mrs. White, hold your fire," Mr. Green said, blocking the kitchen door. "They might be fertile eggs. This is an expensive bird. Three or four eggs resulting in chicks would be a windfall. Please, I beg of you, be patient. At least until we've gotten the eggs and a new buyer lined up."

The bird plucked the feathers from Mrs. Peacock's hat and stuffed them in the fronds of the silver chandelier.

"That's my hat it's destroying," Mrs. Peacock pointed out. She waggled a finger at the bird. "Here, give that back. Find some grass or twigs like other birds."

"It isn't paying any attention to you, Mother." Miss Scarlet said.

Mrs. Peacock raised an eyebrow. "Perhaps we haven't been properly introduced."

"Try talking to it. Hello birdie, hello birdie." Professor Plum raised his voice into a squeak. "Polly want a cracker?"

"Awk, Hello, my name is Cassandra. Hello, my name is Cassandra. Awk."

"How terribly apt. The bird who speaks and no one listens." Mrs. Peacock watched her hat being industriously defoliated. She could almost bear it if the bird shed a feather or two of its own plumage for her next hat. If she could get close enough, she'd wring its cheeky little neck, and then she'd have plenty of feathers.

The bird shuddered, and a big green blob dropped onto the white damask tablecloth.

"See," Mrs. White shrieked. "See what havoc that monster creates?"

"I quite see your point about removing it from the dining room," Mrs. Peacock said. "Can we entice it back to the conservatory with food?"

"Good idea," Mrs. White said. "I've some cold chips and an old kipper in the kitchen. I'll fetch them."

"So, Green, you reckon she's worth a few quid?" Colonel Mustard asked, tapping the carpet with his riding crop. "Ought we to trundle it off to Kensington Market?"

"Gracious no. You don't sell a bird like that on the street. You sell it with letters, telephone calls, and a few words in the right ears."

"There's something odd about that bird," Professor Plum said. "I feel I've seen one before, only not quite like that."

Mrs. Peacock decided enough was enough. The bird was destroying her hat. She kicked off her shoes, climbed up on the table, and lunged at it. The bird took off in an uproar of feathers. The chandelier swung violently. Mrs. Peacock fell back onto the damask with a handful of blue-green feathers and the tattered remains of her hat. The bird flapped into the passageway, Mrs. White in energetic pursuit.

Miss Scarlet clapped her hands. "That was great fun. Shall we chase the bird to another room? Mother, do you think a milliner can restore your hat?"

Mrs. Peacock looked at the feathers in her hand. They were smudged, and her fingers stained an odd indigo-violet shade. Her hat was beyond recognition. She tossed the hat in the waste basket. "Nothing could help this hat. Where is that bird now?"

"From the commotion, I'd guess it's heading toward the conservatory,"

Professor Plum said. "Do you think we ought to help Mrs. White capture it?"

"Righty-ho, chop-chop," Colonel Mustard said. "Onward, gentlemen."

He led a charge down the hall with his riding crop held high. Mr. Green, Professor Plum, and Miss Scarlet hurried after him. Mrs. Peacock took another glance at her hands and the blue feathers, and followed.

Ahead, she could see the bird sailing down the passageway, past paintings of naval battles, to the conservatory. Mrs. White slashed at its tail with her duster. Colonel Mustard's parade was mere footsteps behind. She ought to catch up before any further calamities befell.

She slipped into the conservatory on the heels of Mr. Green. The bird landed on the top of its cage. Mrs. White slammed the conservatory door. "That's enough freedom for that demon. Nobody leaves this room until it's in the cage or dispatched. I fancy a little roasted rare bird for dinner."

"Just a moment, Mrs. White." Mrs. Peacock marched over to John Boddy's body and picked up the paper that had fallen out when the bird had stolen the handkerchief from his pocket. It was a bill of sale for one rare bird, with an astronomical sum marked "Paid."

"This bird is an imposter," she said, holding out her hands and the freshly snatched feathers.

Professor Plum pulled out his magnifying glass and examined her hands and feathers. He hummed, nodded, and turned to consider the bird, preening itself with its lethal-looking beak.

"That's not a Kamehameha Cacatua from Hawaii. I dare say there is no such bird," Professor Plum said. "It's a Psittacus Erithacus. It's a parrot, a Congo African Grey. A plain old garden-variety talking parrot."

"Someone's dyed its feathers to pass it off as something rare." Mrs. Peacock pointed across the room with a smudged blue-green feather. "I accuse you of killing John Boddy in the conservatory with the lead pipe."

BIRDS
OF A
FEATHER

SOLUTION:

Mr. Green stood tall. "I did no such thing. John Boddy paid me fair and square for that bird. If it lays eggs, he can sell them and the bird to the next dupe, I mean, client, and walk away with a profit. Why would I kill him? The deal was done."

"But this bird is an imposter." Mrs. Peacock displayed her stained hands.

"Mr. Boddy didn't know that. It's dashed difficult to get hold of that beast."

"Mr. Boddy did know. He had dye on his hands. He'd managed to grasp it."

"That doesn't prove anything."

"We have proof. We have a witness. The bird. Let's ask it, shall we?" Mrs. Peacock turned to the bird and imitated Mr. Boddy's voice as best as she was able. "This bird's a fake."

"Awk. Still worth plenty, still worth plenty, sell it fast, lots of buyers." The bird's words sounded just like Mr. Green's voice.

Mrs. Peacock changed her voice again, copying the bird. "Sell it fast, lots of buyers."

"Awk. Suppose you're right. Keep it. Few weeks. Dye it again." Mr. Boddy's voice, through the bird.

"There," Mr. Green said. "The witness has spoken. Mr. Boddy and I came to an understanding."

Mrs. Peacock frowned. The bird frowned back at her. She tried again, sounding like Mr. Boddy. "Keep it for a few weeks."

"Awk. Not in my house. Dirty bird." The bird sounded like Mrs. White. "Whack. Arrgghh."

"So it was you, Mrs. White." Mrs. Peacock took out a hanky and dabbed at the stain on her fingers. "You killed Mr. Boddy because he planned to keep the bird and let it fly freely in the house. You hate messes."

Mrs. White stepped to the glass double doors that led from the conservatory to the garden. She swung them open.

The bird swooped past her into the sunshine. It landed in a yew tree, squawked, and flew off into the oak woods.

"There, then, that's your witness taken care of. The first good rain and he'll pass for a raven. I don't mind a bird in a cage, but not a great hulking vulture like that flying around the rooms dropping his gooey green business on every surface. The mess I've had to clean up since Master Boddy opened that cage door. And him thinking to keep it."

As Time
Goes By

11:30 P.M.

Mrs. White hustled toward the kitchen in her nightgown. Time for her late-night snack from the secret stash of shortbread in the pantry. Greedy guests, they'd eat the lot if she put it all on the silver tray. She paused in the doorway, pressed against the door frame. There was someone in the kitchen, bending over near the sink. Was it a burglar? She could only make out a dark shape. The intruder straightened up, scurried on silent feet across the tiled floor and disappeared through the secret passage down into the cellar.

She sneaked up to the secret door and closed it. For good measure, she propped a chair against it. There, let the burglar spend the night wandering around in the cellar in the dark. She'd let him out in the morning.

Why was she here? Oh yes, the shortbread. Pull out a biscuit or two from the top pantry shelf, certain no one was watching. A few steps from door to pantry and she was on her way back to bed with her treasure.

12:15 A.M.

Miss Scarlet wandered into the kitchen. It was dimly lit by the reflections of the passageway lights. Boring, boring, boring house companions. They had all gone to bed and left her at loose ends. Even John Boddy had made his excuses an hour ago, muttering something about wanting a bit of cheese. She wasn't even tired, had nothing to do, and no one to entertain with her exploits in the theatre. She was far more interesting than that stuffy old colonel, with his repetitive war stories.

Drat. John Boddy was sprawled on the kitchen floor in front of the sink, surrounded by broken glass. His head didn't look right, maybe a bump or a gash or a caved-in bit. It was hard to tell in this light. There was something dark beside him, maybe a knife or a wrench or a lead pipe or a candlestick. She nudged it with her toe and it slid under Boddy's arm.

Oh no, she was getting glass shards in her evening slippers. They'd be ruined. She backed up, feeling bits of glass digging into the soles. If she wasn't careful her feet would be cut to ribbons. She tiptoed to the kitchen door, removed her slippers, and carried them upstairs. At least now she had something to do for an hour in her room, not that leafing through catalogues looking for new brushed leather slippers was exciting or interesting, but there you are.

1:15 A.M.

Professor Plum followed the beam of his torch into the kitchen. It reminded him of creeping down tunnels in the pyramids, his throat parched, following that dim beam until he happened on a dusty pile of golden artifacts. Crunching through gravel and sand, anticipation mounting.

What was this dusty pile at his feet in front of the sink? A body. Not a mummy, as it wasn't wrapped. It was wearing a black suit. John Boddy, lying in a pool of something crunchy. He picked up a large shard. Glass. No, crystal. It seemed like the base of something, about three inches in diameter, with curved sides. He should have put on his glasses.

He could hone his detecting skills on this fragment. Waterford, turn of the century, large curved piece, possibly a fruit bowl or tureen or part of a chandelier. Why would Boddy be standing at the sink with a chandelier? Because there was secret treasure inside the chandelier bowl, and he had to break it to extract the goods. What could it be? Gold, most likely, or diamonds. Or pearls, or emeralds, or rubies, the potential list was lengthy.

He should scoop up some of the other fragments, take them upstairs, and examine them under a decent light, with his glasses on. He may have stumbled on a cache of diamonds. What would the British Museum say if his name appeared on the front page of the papers? He could see it now. *Professor Peter Plum Perceives Purloined Precious Pearls.* They'd have to be purloined, or why hide them in a chandelier? The Museum would give him his old job back, with a raise.

But first, he must examine the fragments closely in his room. Why was he down here in the first place? Oh yes, he was thirsty. Better look elsewhere for a tap.

2:15 A.M.

Colonel Mustard felt his way into the kitchen, tapping with his riding crop. The curse of being an old man. If he wasn't up in the night with his waterworks, he was up with heartburn or insomnia. Tonight it was all three in succession. A drink of warm milk might be just the ticket to soothe him into sleep, or a scone, to soak up the heartburn. Despite the dim moonlight he didn't turn on a light. Mrs. White kept the kitchen shipshape. He felt along the cupboards until he reached the scone tin. Proof he didn't need glasses. He could navigate perfectly.

If he wasn't mistaken, there was something on the floor in the corner by the sink. Bad form, rubbish on the floor. No, it wasn't rubbish, it was

John Boddy. Bit of a sticky wicket there. Broken glass on the tiles. Ought not to venture further. He reached out with his riding crop and poked. No response. Man must be dead. Only explanation for lying in a heap like that in the middle of the night beside the sink.

Task at hand for this man's army. Summon the authorities. Clear the area.

Dash, this heartburn was a bother. Ought to see to it first. Can't take command without feeling prime. A scone or two, a cup of milk, taken in his room in his nice warm bed. Made him feel sleepy just thinking about it.

First order of business, then. Deal with the heartburn and the insomnia, then address this new situation later. Much later. Lie in bed and devise a strategy. Indeed.

3:15 A.M.

Mr. Green slithered into the kitchen through the rear door, dusting off his hands. Now it had risen above the trees, the full moon provided perfect lighting for the heist. The study hadn't coughed up much, just a bit of brass. He'd nicked some good loot in the lounge, thanks to that Peacock woman always pointing out the better quality objets d'art, and Professor Plum rhyming off the provenance of antiquities. The passageways were littered with swag. There was so much moveable boodle here he'd be set for the next six months. Blessed are those who help themselves, for they shall not have to share the profits.

John Boddy lay crumpled in the corner. Must be dead or he would be up in his room, rubbing his head and ribs wondering what happened. Mr. Green paused beside him to check for vital signs. Nothing.

That put the kibosh on topping off his spree with silverware. The police would be all over the kitchen, and the missing kit would be exposed. Blessed are those who plan ahead, foreseeing the need to hide the booty under the garden until the policemen retreated. A bit of dirt never hurt a bottle of rare wine or a brass paperweight.

Off to bed then, to dream of pawnbrokers and privatte collectors.

4:15 A.M.

Mrs. Peacock slipped silently into the kitchen. She was famished. Mrs. White's impossible meals and the necessity of resorting to toast for dinner led to hunger pangs in the middle of the night. What could she scrounge up tonight? The shortbread would be all gone; Professor Plum always attacked it with relish. There might be some chocolate, or biscuits, or a big wedge of cheese and chunk of fresh bread. Something she could eat without needing dishes, so no one would be the wiser about her midnight raid.

She nearly tripped over John Boddy. What an unappetizing sight. It made her feel quite squeamish. Or perhaps that was the hunger. She ought to summon the colonel. He would know what to do about such matters. But why bother at this hour? It could wait until morning. Besides, how could she explain her presence in the kitchen, when by day she claimed to be sufficiently fed on two lettuce leaves and a radish? Ah, here, an orange, some cheese already sliced on the drain board, and a handful of strawberries. Perfect.

She slipped back out of the kitchen toward her room.

5:15 A.M.

Mrs. White smoothed her apron as she entered the kitchen. The chair was still up against the secret passage door, but she'd deal with that problem when she had the colonel beside her, with his knowledge of fighting.

On to the task at hand. First things first. The chopped oranges and lemons had been soaking all night for marmalade. It meant an early start today, what with having to boil down the soaked fruit and put it in jars. Once the marmalade was boiling, she could grate the cheese for the Welsh rarebit and prepare the Ardentinny Drop bannocks. Rather a lot of cheese needed for the rarebit, perhaps she could cut back, substitute something. Her mother's recipe called for eggs, milk and cheese beaten together and cooked in a pot until wobbly-firm, like scrambled eggs. Maybe she could use flour to thicken instead. One or two eggs, a dollop of flour, milk, a sprinkle of cheese—that might be too thick to cook in a pot. She could fry it instead. Shape it into patties. Good idea.

She stepped into the pantry for the cheese. It was gone. She stepped back in the kitchen. There was something orange on the far counter near the sink. Had someone eaten all the cheese? Or had it rolled on the floor? A quick dust-off and it would be fine.

But what was this, slumped on the floor in front of the sink? Master John, and it looked like someone had given him a right clobber on the noggin. Dirty footprints around him. Crumbs on the counter. Broken glass all over the floor. He must have been getting a drink of water at the sink. She'd have to give the floor a good sweep or she'd be cutting her feet, and how could she do the rooms wearing ruddy great foot dressings?

Sweep, sweep, sweep. Glass had a way of tossing itself a distance. All those little shards that resisted the broom. She found a damp rag and wiped them up, taking great care not to cut her hands. Half an hour, that's what that business took. And her with marmalade on the boil and the bannocks not started.

Well, toss it. Why was she bothering anyway, with this crowd and their noses turned up at all her best dishes? She should just go back to bed and sleep to a normal hour. She pulled the marmalade pot off the Aga cooker and set it in the pantry.

Let them eat toast. With last week's jam.

8:04 A.M.

How could matters get much worse? Her best china cream and sugar were missing. Mrs. White piled the toast on the tray with the tea and swung into the dining room. They were all gathered around the table, well, all except Miss Scarlet who rarely dragged herself out of bed much before noon. Time to have it out with them. One of them had meddled in her kitchen and she wasn't going to stand for it.

"Good morning all. I trust you slept well."

"Quite," Mrs. Peacock said.

"Like a baby," Mr. Green said.

"Touch of heartburn. Old man's complaint." Colonel Mustard tapped his chest.

"I remember being thirsty," Professor Plum said. "Must have been too much salt on the sliced bananas we had for dessert last night."

"Was anyone in the kitchen during the night?" she asked, pouring tea in china cups and passing them around.

"Not I," Colonel Mustard said. "No need for it, you see. Don't cook."

"Nor I," Mrs. Peacock said. "Why would I visit the kitchen in the night?"

"I went to bed and slept soundly," Professor Plum said. "Never left my room."

"Same here," Mr. Green said. "Comfortable bed, why leave it?"

Mrs. White placed a platter of dry cold toast on the table. "Sorry, just toast and tea this morning. The kitchen is a bit of a shambles, what with

Master Boddy being killed and all. The policemen will be here momentarily, so if you've need of a second cup, speak up now and I'll put the kettle on again."

Every single one of them gasped. Mrs. Peacock's hand flew to her throat. Professor Plum dropped his glasses. Mr. Green ran a hand through his thinning hair. Colonel Mustard clutched his row of medals.

"That's that then," Mrs. White said. "I'll refresh the tea, shall I?" She picked up her tray and returned to the kitchen. Lying through their teeth, they were. One of them had been in this kitchen and done Master Boddy a trouncer. She'd do a little snooping.

11:15 A.M.

Mrs. White carried the silver coffee tray into the lounge. They were all there, waiting like vultures to pounce on the scones. Even Miss Scarlet was present, sprawled on the chintz chesterfield in an ermine-trimmed rose satin dressing gown.

"Good morning, Miss Scarlet," she said. "Did you sleep well? Or did you have to visit the kitchen in the night?" She put the tray on the small table and poured five cups.

"Yes, and no. Is that coffee? I must have coffee."

"The policemen weren't going to let me in the kitchen at all, but when I mentioned coffee, they reckoned I might as well come in, seeing as they were parched with the morning's effort. So here's a full pot, and scones beside."

Mrs. Peacock straightened her powder blue skirt over her knees. "Why are you so interested in our night habits, Mrs. White? Is something missing from the kitchen?"

"Funny you should ask." Mrs. White left the room and returned with another tray. 'I asked each of you if you'd been in the kitchen last night, and each of you said no. After breakfast, I went upstairs to make up the beds. Here are a few things I found."

Professor Plum leaned forward in his seat. "Are we going to play Kim's Game, where you show us the tray and then take something off it and we have to guess what's missing?"

"No, it's not a game. I have here," she pointed to each item in turn, "a bit of broken glass, a muddy shoe, a damaged slipper, some orange peels, and an empty milk glass."

She never saw such a medley of blushes and embarrassed glances.

"There is also the matter of the chair against the secret passage door, the Waterford crystal, and the candlestick. Not to mention the cheese crumbs on the drain board and the kitchen knife sticking out between Master Boddy's shoulder blades. I want to know who killed Master Boddy."

"The authorities will sort it all out, never you fear." Colonel Mustard tapped his riding crop against his boot for emphasis.

"That may be, but I've a kitchen that's been violated. I'll tell you what I have here."

She pointed at each item on her tray. "This piece of broken glass was in your room, Professor. It is part of the Waterford broken on the floor around Master Boddy. This pink slipper has bits of glass in the sole. The wearer walked through the glass on the kitchen floor. I think we all know who wears pink slippers here." She glared at Miss Scarlet. "I found this muddy shoe in Mr. Green's room, under the bed. There are muddy footprints on the kitchen floor from the back door to the passageway. I found this milk glass in Colonel Mustard's room, and these orange peels in Mrs. Peacock's room."

"Excellent work, Mrs. White," Mrs. Peacock said. "You've proven we were all in the kitchen at one time or other. How does that solve the problem?"

"It makes me wonder, why did you all lie about it?" She stared at each of them in turn. They stared down at their coffee cups. "You lied because Master Boddy was already dead when you visited. I was in the kitchen myself early on, and saw a burglar sneak into the cellar through the secret passage."

"That solves it, then," Miss Scarlet said. "The burglar killed him."

"I put a chair against the door, and the chair is still there. So the burglar must have let himself out in the study. There are a few things missing throughout the house."

"Confirming the burglar theory," Mr. Green said.

"One is a candlestick from the dining room. The other half of the pair is under Master Boddy. Another is Sir Hugh's Waterford crystal polo trophy, also from the dining room. It's broken all over the kitchen floor. Most importantly, the cheese is missing."

"The cheese? How can cheese be important?" Professor Plum asked.

"Master Boddy was in the kitchen getting himself a snack. He had sliced the cheese on the drain board. Someone took the cheese."

"I was hungry," Mrs. Peacock said. "Is that a crime?"

"No, but Master Boddy sliced the cheese with the knife, and now the knife is stuck in his back."

"Well, now we're really getting somewhere." Mrs. Peacock threw her hands up in mock exasperation. "That explains everything."

"No need to be uppity, Mrs. Peacock. I've more to say on the matter."

"It rather sounds like a giant jigsaw puzzle," Professor Plum said. "Do you have all the pieces?"

"I believe I do," Mrs. White said. She stepped out of the room and came back brandishing a muddy shovel. "I accuse you of killing Master Boddy in the kitchen with the knife."

As Time Goes By

Solution:

She pointed the shovel at Mr. Green.

"I believe the burglar picked up the crystal bowl and the pair of candlesticks in the dining room. When he moved to the kitchen, he was surprised by Master Boddy, making himself a snack. Master Boddy grabbed the candlestick. The burglar fought back and whacked him on the head with the bowl. The bowl fell and smashed. The burglar grabbed the knife and stabbed Master Boddy. Master Boddy fell at the sink, still holding the candlestick. The burglar picked up his remaining loot and slipped away down the secret passage. I blocked the entrance. It didn't matter, because the burglar had no intention of coming back that way. He went past the wine cellar and resurfaced in the study. There he found a few more things to steal. I'm sure when I take an inventory, I'll know what's missing."

"Kim's Game. I knew we could play." Professor Plum smiled.

"When the burglar finished his work, he went outside and buried the lot so the police wouldn't find it when they investigated the murder. I dare say there'll be a freshly turned spot in the vegetable garden. Too bad he didn't realize his shoes were muddy when he finished."

Mr. Green looked down at his feet. "Blessed are those who remember to wipe their feet at the door, for they shall not be found out."

"Here, Professor," Mrs. White said, handing Professor Plum the shovel. "You're an archeologist. I want my china back, unbroken. You know a lot about digging."

ALL THE
TEA IN
CHINA

Down the passageway, Mrs. White could see the Colonel, taking revolvers off the wall, examining them, and replacing them. It looked like he was searching for a particular model, but as long as he put them all back, she'd leave him to it.

Mrs. White carried the silver tea tray into the conservatory where the guests were collected for elevenses. Mrs. Peacock had suggested the conservatory this morning as the sun was streaming in the large windows, making the geraniums glow. They had fallen in with her notion like sheep.

Too bad they were like sheep instead of wolves when it came to breakfast. Leaving saucy plates, breakfast half eaten, they were then expecting scones or shortbread with their coffee. If they'd fill up at the table with porridge and blood pudding, she wouldn't have to do this extra round of baking.

Today she'd made Pitcaithly bannocks, and here they were, pouncing on them as if they'd had no breakfast at all. She had no opportunity to pass the plate in an orderly fashion.

Mr. Green took a handful with a moan of pleasure. "Blessed are the bannocks, for they are as manna from Heaven," he said, cramming one into his mouth with pudgy fingers.

"Oh, I say, these look splendid," Professor Plum said, picking two and eyeing a third.

The ladies were slightly more genteel, but Mrs. Peacock elbowed her way to the plate ahead of her daughter. Even Miss Scarlet, who surely must be watching her figure, like all the young ladies, took two.

A moment later, Colonel Mustard hurried in. "Am I too late?" He looked relieved on spotting the plate of bannocks and scooped up a clutch.

In the silence following the plate, Mrs. White began pouring tea into the Royal Worcester cups.

"What? Tea? Where's the coffee?" Miss Scarlet screeched. "We always have coffee at elevenses. I live for coffee."

"Sorry, Miss, but I was that busy making bannocks and scraping plates I didn't have time to grind the coffee beans." Mrs. White poured another cup and offered it to her. "Tea?"

Colonel Mustard perched on the stone ledge of the fountain, an arm's length from the plate. "Buck up, Miss Scarlet. The tea will wash down the bannock just as well as coffee. Just like a revolver is as good as a pistol when you've a place to hang it on the wall, right, Boddy?"

John Boddy stood near the doorway, ignoring the bannocks and declining tea. He did not answer the colonel.

"I want coffee. I want coffee." Miss Scarlet stamped her foot.

Mrs. Peacock commandeered the chaise longue. "Don't prattle on so, Josephine. There'll be coffee tomorrow. We'll forgo the blood pudding and settle for toast, so Mrs. White will have time to deal with the coffee beans."

Professor Plum and Mr. Green took chairs beside the aspidistra. "I say, that's a capital idea, Mrs. Peacock," Professor Plum said. "Toast and tea, then scones and coffee."

Miss Scarlet fluttered onto a bench near the fish tank. "I shall die without coffee. I shall just die."

"Delightful flavor," Mrs. Peacock said, sipping. "Is this Earl Gray?"

"No, it's Assam," Professor Plum said. "Full-bodied, brisk, and malty."

Mrs. Peacock raised an eyebrow.

"The professor's right, he is," Mrs. White said. "Assam, and I've a chest full of it in the cellar."

"Didn't we have this last night after dinner?" Colonel Mustard asked.

"No, that was Darjeeling," Professor Plum said. "Smooth with a muscatel flavor and a delicate aftertaste."

"How do you know so much about it?" Miss Scarlet asked, pouting at her cup as she stirred with a tiny silver spoon.

"My father, Chauncey Plum, is a tea merchant. He tested teas daily when we lived in Egypt. Mum Plum always had the kettle on."

"I remember Chauncey," Colonel Mustard said, smoothing his moustache. "Quite an astute businessman, as I recall. Did rather well for himself and Snively, his business partner. Quite a shock when Chauncey was lost at sea. Swept overboard by a rogue wave. Snively was dashed lucky, as he'd been on deck at the time, and saved himself by clinging to the mast." He reached for another bannock. "1898, if I'm not mistaken."

Professor Plum gasped. "No! Really? Oh, I say. I had no idea. I was only ten, and was not advised of the details. Mum Plum and I went home to England when Papa Plum didn't come home. Mum said he'd gone off to America in a special ship and wouldn't be back for a few years. I was never quite sure what had happened. Oh, I am most overcome." Professor Plum put down his cup and fumbled in his pockets for a handkerchief.

"Now, then, buck up, lad," Mrs. White said. "He's been gone these many years. Have another cup of tea. It will perk you right up." She refilled his cup. "Colonel, you were having a look at the antique revolver collection. Searching for anything in particular? Master Boddy keeps a record of the collections." She turned to the doorway for confirmation, but Master Boddy had gone.

"No, nothing of the sort. Just interested. Bit of a collector myself. Have a few specimens on order. Rather a long wait."

"It must be dicey, buying antique guns. I hear people smuggle them into the country," Miss Scarlet said.

Colonel Mustard turned his back on her. "There now, Plum's got himself sorted, haven't you, old chap? Shape up or ship out, I always say. Snively himself related the incident to me the following year. I'm sure your mother was informed. Children ought to be seen and not hear details, I always say. Many things are said in a household that are no concern of the children's."

Miss Scarlet frowned. "You must have come into money, if your father left the business solvent. Surely that was a clue, when your mother took you to the sweet shop and let you have whatever you wanted."

Professor Plum shook his head. "It was never like that. We struggled on Mum Plum's wages from three jobs. We never had a whisper of Papa Plum's earnings."

"Did you not think that odd?" Mrs. Peacock asked.

"Not while I was a child, no," Professor Plum said. "Mum Plum managed to put me through grammar school and I won a scholarship at Oxford. When I graduated and began lecturing, I got wondering about what happened to Papa's business interests. In 1911, I decided to track Snively down and see about taking over Papa's portion of the business. I was ready to make a career of it."

"Did you find him?" Miss Scarlet asked, swinging her shoe on one toe.

"I found Snively had sold Papa Plum's share of the business to Sir Hugh Black in 1904. Snively had continued to run it profitably, I'm told. Snively sold the rest of the business to Sir Hugh in 1910. Shortly afterward, Snively died."

"Well then, that's all above board," Mr. Green said. "Sir Hugh paid Snively for Chauncey's portion, and the money came to your mother."

"But Snively never paid Mum. I sat on a bench beside Snively's grave, working it all out. I still thought Papa lived in America, running some new venture, but the business he left behind had been sold, before Snively died. Someone owed us money."

"How intriguing," Mrs. Peacock said. "What did you do?"

"When I returned home, I visited Sir Hugh. He said he had set Papa's portion of the company aside in trust for me when I came of age. He'd just forgotten to track me down." Professor Plum frowned. "I was well over age by then, and could have used the money when I was in studying."

"It must have been a modest business. Sir Hugh didn't spend much time operating his companies," Colonel Mustard said. "Without a firm hand at the helm, I'm sure sales dwindled."

"They do a brisk trade in tea, if the tea chests in the cellar are any indication," Mrs. White said. "Go and see for yourself, Professor. They land in here regular as clockwork. I use the wrench to open the crates. It seems to work as well as a crowbar, and is smaller to handle."

"No need to bother, dear boy." Colonel Mustard cleared his throat. "A few tea chests in the cellar of the company's owner are no indication of the success of the company. It could be just the last few chests they couldn't sell. I'll go and count them for you, shall I?"

"Nevertheless, there would have been some money if Sir Hugh took the trouble to set up a trust fund," Mrs. Peacock said.

"Yes, there was," Professor Plum said. "In lieu of payment, Sir Hugh offered to fund my archeological expeditions. He said that would cost far more than what he owed me. I was at loose ends for the summer term, so I took him up on it. Twenty years of expeditions, he promised me. I couldn't go during the Great War. I've only made six trips. I intend to renegotiate with Mr. Boddy. I suppose I ought to tell him Papa Plum was lost at sea."

Professor Plum stared morosely into his cup. Mrs. Peacock coughed and left the room. Mr. Green checked his watch, looked surprised, and hurried away.

Colonel Mustard glanced out the window. "Fine day for a stroll in the gardens," he said, and marched into the passageway.

Miss Scarlet eyed the plate. "I'll eat the last one for you, Mrs. White. No point in throwing it out." She scooped up the last bannock and wandered away, dropping crumbs at every step.

Mrs. White cleared the empty cups onto her silver tray and took them back to the kitchen, leaving Professor Plum to his melancholy. The counter was heaped with the breakfast dishes. She'd her work cut out for her. The secret passageway door to the cellar hung slightly ajar. Someone must be downstairs.

Half an hour later she picked up her feather duster and began the rounds. The conservatory was empty. She polished the fish tank with a quick swipe of her elbow and wafted Miss Scarlet's crumbs into the pot of the split-leaf philodendron.

She continued down the passageway, polishing candlesticks here, dusting marble statuettes there, until she reached the library. It needed seeing to. Why couldn't guests put books back on the shelves when they were done with them? Slovenly habits. A newspaper here, an old book there, it was enough to make you weep.

She picked up the open book on the library table. A yellowed piece of paper fell out of it. The paper displayed a handwritten scrawl. She closed the book. The paper did not belong inside the book, she was sure. It must belong to one of the guests. Which one? She read it.

The Deathbed Statement of Able Seaman Buntford.

They tell me I'm dying, and I ought to cleanse my soul before I meet the Almighty. I remember one incident well, in 1898. It was a choppy day on the Atlantic. I was in the galley, coming to the deck for my watch. Sure as I peeked out the porthole, I saw the two passengers, Plum and Snively, arguing on the forward deck. A bit of a wave hit, a foot-wetter, splashed over the deck. Plum was wearing slippery shoes and he lost his footing and fell against his companion. Snively took the opportunity and heaved Plum overboard. Fearing the look on Snively's face, and the fact I was headed to my watch with an illegal bottle of rum concealed on my person, I chose not to speak out. I ran back to the Captain and reported a man overboard, then slipped out to my watch post. In the confusion, I was able to stash my bottle. The Captain called all hands to save Plum, but we never saw him surface. I completed my watch and was three sails to the wind when I retired to my bed, so I didn't hear Snively's story about the rogue wave washing Plum to his death. I long wondered why he wasn't brought to justice, thinking he would have admitted his guilt in a fit of remorse. 'Twas a fine bottle Snively provided me with the next day, and many fine ones since. And that's what I wish to cleanse my soul of, my weakness for rum, and all the times I carried out my duties with a bottle at hand. May the Lord forgive me for this failing.

She tucked the paper in her pocket. The professor would be interested in reading it. In the passageway she saw Professor Plum and Colonel Mustard ahead of her. Before she could catch up, Professor Plum entered the study and Colonel Mustard continued to the lounge.

Mrs. White dusted her way down the passageway to the study. "Professor? I've something you might be interested in."

The secret passage door was slightly ajar in this room, too, and Professor Plum had disappeared. She shrugged and tucked the paper away. She could give it to him at dinner.

She dusted the desk and the globe, and was sweeping the ashes off the hearth when she noticed a note on crisp letterhead fluttering in the draft on the floor behind the door. She picked it up and read it as she carried it to the wastebasket.

You, Sir, are a bounder and a cad. Thrice I paid you for deliverable goods, and thrice you failed to deliver. An aborted shipment, you say. I say, return my money then, forthwith. If I have not received adequate recompense by the end of the year, I shall, at my earliest convenience, visit you and exact my due.

Perhaps she ought to keep it. She tucked the note in her apron pocket. Master Boddy was doing some kind of historical research about money, allowances and the guests now at the mansion. He might be interested in filing this with the rest of his papers.

In the front hall she gave the suit of armor the once-over with the feather duster and carried on into the lounge. Colonel Mustard was not there, and the secret door to the cellar was open. There must be quite a crowd in the cellar by now. Perhaps one of them would be kind enough to bring up some spuds for dinner.

When she returned to the kitchen, she found John Boddy sprawled on the floor, a wrench to his left and a slip of paper under his hand showing a long list of numbers. She shouted for help. Running footsteps echoed down all the passageways.

Guests spilled into the room. Mrs. Peacock, lips clenched, gripped a fashion magazine and glanced at her watch. Miss Scarlet pirouetted into a chair, as if she was waiting to be entertained. Professor Plum glared daggers at Colonel Mustard. Colonel Mustard's bushy eyebrows met in consternation, and he had little black flakes stuck to his sleeves from the cuffs to the elbows. Mr. Green held forth an empty teacup with hope in his eyes.

Mrs. White threatened them all with her feather duster. "What's going on here, I'd like to know? What are you all doing running around in the cellar, and what's Master Boddy doing lying dead on my clean kitchen floor?"

Mrs. Peacock gasped and dropped her magazine. Miss Scarlet leaned forward with interest.

"I saw the Colonel in the cellar with the wrench, rooting through the tea chests, scattering tea everywhere," Professor Plum said, straightening his glasses on his nose. "Do you know how valuable tea leaves are, sir? You can't fling them on the floor and sweep them up, expecting to get a decent cup out of them."

"There are things you don't know about the importation of those tea chests." Colonel Mustard pulled himself up to attention. "I saw the Professor in the cellar, opening the tea chests with the wrench, sniffing the contents, and making notes on a scrap of paper."

"Would this be the note?" Mrs. White asked, plucking the scrap of paper from Master Boddy's cold hand.

"Indeed it would."

"That is an estimate of the value of the tea in the chests," Professor

Plum said. "I believe half of it belongs to me, as the benefactor of my father's estate. It's a good starting point in repaying me what's owed."

"The tea's here because Sir Hugh did business with Chauncey Plum and Mr. Snively," Mrs. White said. "When Chauncey Plum was lost at sea, Mr. Snively took over the company. Sir Hugh smelled a rat. It takes one to know one, I say. Anyroad, Sir Hugh did some investigating." She pulled a paper from her pocket and placed it flat on the table. "Sir Hugh turned up a sailor who'd happened to be on his way up from the hold when the rogue wave hit. He said it was no more than a tall wave that skittered over the deck, a foot-wetter, he called it. But he saw Mr. Snively push Chauncey Plum overboard."

Miss Scarlet gasped.

"I'll tell you one thing," Mrs. White said. "There's importing tea and there's smuggling. I accuse you of killing Master Boddy in the kitchen with the wrench."

ALL THE
TEA IN
CHINA

SOLUTION:

Both Professor Plum and Colonel Mustard shouted at once. "I did not."

Mrs. White pointed at the colonel. "You made a deal with Sir Hugh to smuggle antique revolvers into the country in tea chests. You carried on the deal with Master Boddy. But you weren't getting the revolvers and he wasn't paying any attention to the matter. So there you were, rummaging through the tea, up to your elbows in tea leaves, once you found out where the tea chests were."

Colonel Mustard nodded. "Yes, that's true. But I didn't kill Boddy. I met him in the cellar and he told me the shipments didn't materialize, and there was nothing I could do but accept my losses with good grace. I went back to the lounge, in a high temper, I must say."

"But you, Professor, found out today that your father was murdered," Mrs. White continued. "Both Sir Hugh and Master Boddy knew about it, but hadn't seen fit to tell you. I don't think Mr. Snively sold your father's share of the business to Sir Hugh. I think Sir Hugh took it from him in lieu of letting the world know how Chauncey Plum died. Master Boddy had no such reason for keeping quiet, with all parties dead. But he did, because of the money. If he didn't tell you the truth, he could keep the profits from the business."

"But—"

"You discovered that today in the library." Mrs. White pointed to the sailor's deathbed confession. "You found out you had been robbed of your inheritance first by Mr. Snively, then Sir Hugh, and finally Master Boddy."

Professor Plum sighed. "They all knew about my father. That evil Snively, the grasping Sir Hugh, and cheapskate John Boddy. Sir Hugh kept my father's fate from me, and ruined all my plans for a career as a tea merchant. He fobbed me off with the promise of trips abroad, but I see now my father's business was worth far more. Mr. Boddy said he didn't intend to tell me about Papa Plum, and I had no rights to any of the profits from the company, since he was under no obligation to honor Sir Hugh's commitments. I followed him up the steps, the wrench still in my hand, and whacked him."

"That's all well and good," Colonel Mustard said, "but I'm still missing my antique revolvers."

Mrs. White stepped to one of the cupboards and opened a drawer, releasing a strong smoky tea aroma, and displaying a jumble of guns dusted with tea leaves. "Is this what you're after, Colonel? I visit the chests every day for fresh tea and I kept finding these. What kind of careless person puts a grubby old gun in a chest of clean tea?"

HEADS UP

Mr. Green stalked the passageways of Tudor Hall, looking for something to nick. Blessed are the nimble of finger, for they shall be rewarded at the pawn shop. There was a smorgasbord of potential objects that would fetch a few bob on Portobello Road. A bit below his usual standards, working in small change, but it kept him amused. The trick here was to select the correct object, one that was worth something, would not be missed, and was easy to conceal in a pocket.

The pewter seagull looked promising, particularly if he moved a few things around on the table, pulling the silver butterfly to the fore, pushing the copper scarab back, and shifting the china dog to the left. There. That made a smashing new bit of ornamentation.

Apparently he wasn't the only one examining the merchandise. Just inside the door of the billiard room, John Boddy, Mrs. Peacock, Colonel Mustard, and Mrs. White were standing staring up. Had he missed a gilt ceiling? Or had they found the Cobweb to End All Cobwebs?

"What are all these abominations?" Mrs. Peacock asked.

"They're the trophies from the safari Sir Hugh Black and his father went on in 1892," Colonel Mustard said. "Old Black died on that trip. Dreadful business. Shot by an elephant gun. Accidents often happen on safari. Bull elephant charging, twenty men armed and shooting, chaos, people running in all directions. We didn't bag the elephant. It destroyed the tents, though. When the elephant had gone, the old man was dead. Rather put the kibosh on the trip."

"Is this what Hugh brought home? Trophies? Rows of shaggy heads with horns?"

"Yes, that's a warthog, that's a gnu, that's an impala. Sir Hugh shot the impala, couldn't miss, there were over a thousand of them thundering past. He'd only to shoot in their general direction. Too bad he hit a female, with no horns." Colonel Mustard rocked back on his heels. "That one is a tsessebe, fastest member of the African antelope family. I bagged it myself. I'm a crack shot, you see. I took down the gnu, too. Dashed difficult to shoot, gnus."

"So these trophies have hung here for thirty-four years?" Mrs. Peacock asked. "No wonder they're so dusty. This room is in sore need of redecorating, if it's been like this for three decades."

"Oh, you couldn't possibly take them down," Colonel Mustard said. "It's a shrine, you see, to Sir Hugh's father. His last legacy. If you don't count his ashes in an urn in the library."

"Shrine, pah. Mrs. White, ring the locals for some scaffolding. We're going to take them all down." Mrs. Peacock waved her hanky at the hairy beasts as if to ward off their lingering mustiness.

"Take them down and there'll be a row of faded patches on the wall, and then there's a job for me with the emulsion paint. No thank you. I've enough to do. The heads stay up." Mrs. White folded her arms across her apron and stood blocking the door.

Mr. Green watched with amusement as Mrs. White, Mrs. Peacock, and Colonel Mustard argued about the removal of the animal heads. He scanned them, from left to right. Gazelle, warthog, gnu, impala, tsessebe, kudu, oryx. It was a dusty and flea-bitten collection, the heads of slower animals. These were the trophies of lesser hunters. Colonel Mustard had shot the fleet of foot, the desirable antelopes. The other gentlemen had been poor marksmen. They hadn't bagged anything decent, like a lion or tiger.

Above the row of heads a single elephant tusk hung mounted on a polished board. Colonel Mustard had just said the elephant got away, and small wonder, with those incompetent hunters. Someone had probably purchased an old tusk in the village market after the safari ended and they were headed home with nothing to brag about.

John Boddy seemed resigned to the inevitable, that Mrs. Peacock would have her way with the heads. He stood patiently to one side, listening, waiting. Perhaps he had no great love for his grandfather's trophies.

The next morning after breakfast a great clanging and banging rose from the billiard room. Mr. Green arrived at the doorway with a crystal inkwell in his pocket in time to see four seedy workmen assembling a questionable eighteen-foot scaffolding along the wall of trophies. They shuffled past Mr. Boddy, accepted cash with a tip of the hat, and left.

Mrs. Peacock examined their workmanship by grabbing a corner of the structure and shaking. The whole thing clanked and swayed.

"This isn't safe," she said, turning. "Mr. Green, go find a rope so we can tie this together. Professor Plum, go and find a hammer and some nails."

As he left on his mission, Mr. Green passed Mrs. White, who was staring at the arrangement of bric-a-brac on the sideboard and shaking her head. She moved them all back to their correct places. He hastened his steps to the kitchen, found a rope in the pantry, and tucked the crystal inkwell into the potato bin. Playing a game of Moving Fingers against Mrs. White might be more fun than stealing in this house.

Back in the billiard room, he offered Mrs. Peacock the rope.

"Don't just stand there," she said. "Get tying. Find out where the scaffolding is weak and fortify it. You don't want to have it fall apart while you're up there, do you? Where's the professor with the hammer?"

Mr. Green knew he'd been trapped. Not for him idle wandering and innocent theft today. He'd just become an indentured servant to the House of Hoary Heads. He wrapped the rope around two of the uprights and snugged them together with a big knot.

"Are you finished, Mr. Green? Then climb up to the top. Colonel Mustard, you get up on the middle level and be ready to take what Mr. Green hands you. Mr. Boddy, you stand beside the supply cupboard under Colonel Mustard, can you reach from there? Good. We'll hand the heads down in bucket brigade fashion."

Mr. Green chuckled at her use of the word 'we.' Mrs. Peacock had no intention of getting her hands dirty, he was sure. The scaffolding shuddered as Colonel Mustard climbed up.

"Steady on, chaps," Colonel Mustard said. "Green, what are you playing at up there? The whole thing's moving. Too dangerous by half, I'd say. We ought to quit for elevenses and have those men come back and do the job properly. Let them climb their own scaffolding, and then we'll find out what's safe and what's not."

"Nonsense. We'll be finished by elevenses if we start now. Mr. Green? Are you ready?"

"Yes, Mrs. Peacock. What do you want first? The impala or the tsessebe?"

"Start with the topmost. That elephant tusk. Hand it down, there's a dear."

The elephant tusk was mounted on a long oak plaque with brass brackets. He ran his fingers along the ivory. Smooth. And caked with dust. How many piano keys can you carve out of one tusk? This one was monstrous, when you got right up to it. Over ten feet long, by the eyeball. It must be worth a fortune. He inched along to the butt end of the tusk. It was encased in a brass, no, a gold band. Gold. He was positive. He'd handled enough gold in the last few years. If he could gauge the thickness, see if it was solid gold or tempered with another metal—

"What are you frittering with, Mr. Green? We don't have all day. It's almost eleven o'clock."

"Just finding out how it's attached to the wall. Need to grasp it at the right spot."

"It will be hooked at the middle. What are you doing at the end? Go back to the center and lift. Pass it down to Colonel Mustard. He'll pass it down to Mr. Boddy."

Mr. Green shuffled back to the middle of the piece. The scaffolding shuddered and groaned. The rope yawed and squeaked. Colonel Mustard muttered and grumbled.

He tipped the oak slab toward him slightly and felt behind it. Yes, it was hooked to the wall here, although from the resistance he suspected it was hooked in a few other places. Nevertheless, he should be able to lift it clear by moving it straight up, then straight out.

He pushed up. Goodness, it was heavy. How did elephants carry these around all day? The mounting oak slab was hefty in itself, long and thick. He pushed up again. Gracious heavens. He barely moved it.

"Well?" Mrs. Peacock's voice was becoming shrill.

"It's heavier than expected."

"Nonsense. You're a strong man. Put your shoulder to it. Colonel Mustard is poised below you. You've only to swing it to the left when you have it free of the wall."

Mr. Green gave it his shoulder. Blessed are those who wear expensive suits, for their shoulders will be padded. He heard the oak scrape up the wall, and a pinging of sheared nails. He grasped the plaque with both hands and pulled it toward him.

'Struth. It was far too heavy to manage. It would need three men.

Only he'd managed to clear it from the sheared nails, and it was coming down fast, courtesy of his friend Gravity.

He yelped and jumped backward. The tusk crashed past him, bounced on the scaffolding, and followed its heaviest end downward.

"Every man for himself!" Colonel Mustard shouted.

Boddy shouted something, too, but his words were lost under Mrs. Peacock's scream. Mr. Green heard cracking, banging, scrambling, as the mighty tusk shuddered past the scaffolding supports, whacked the gnu, sheared the warts off the warthog, and plunged through the tall window.

Dust billowed. Glass tinkled. Wood groaned. A pair of hands applauded.

"That was a delightful performance," Miss Scarlet said from the doorway. "Can you do it again?"

Mr. Green found himself hanging by one arm from the top level of the scaffolding, swaying in the aftershock. He swung onto the lower level, found his footing, and decided the best way out was to jump to the billiard table.

He sighted the distance from the scaffold to the billiard table. No one was in a position to stop him, particularly if he was quick. He jumped. With a second jump he was on the floor. It was bad form to walk on the host's billiard table, but sometimes these things can't be helped.

Colonel Mustard cowered against the cue rack. Mrs. Peacock was ashen, her hands clamped to her face. Mr. Boddy brushed dust off his jacket and picked up a brittle piece of paper.

"What the devil?" Mrs. White's voice ricocheted through the sudden silence. "What've you gone and done? Taken down the tusk? Look at that faded patch on the wall. Just look. I told you not to take those trophies down. You've caused no end of havoc, haven't you?"

Miss Scarlet clapped her hands again. "Is that coffee? Oh, goody. Let's all go to the lounge for coffee."

"Coffee? I say, did I miss something?" Professor Plum held out a hammer and two nails. He blinked at the scene. "Tried to move the tusk, did you? You need four men for that. I saw them shipping them out in Egypt."

Mrs. Peacock fanned herself with her hanky and followed the coffee tray out of the room.

"Right then, Green, Boddy?" Colonel Mustard said. "Didn't lose a man in that operation, did we? Lost a window, pity. The gnu seems to have lived, minus some of his official provenance. The warthog's the worse for wear. Expect you'll need to telephone a glazier, what?"

John Boddy nodded and carried the brittle piece of paper to his study.

Mr. Green was never so glad to see a hot cup of coffee, even if it was Mrs. White's weak creation. He could have been killed. They all could have been killed. It made a person want to take a stroll in the sunshine and appreciate the finer things. He drained his coffee cup, made his excuses, and pinched an alabaster pineapple on the way out the front door.

The walk to the village did him good. So did the little exchange in the pub, an alabaster pineapple for ten pence, an ice lolly for a treat, and a jingle in his pocket on the way back to the mansion.

Miss Scarlet met him at the door. "Where have you been? John Boddy's been killed. In the billiard room. The scaffolding fell on him."

Mr. Green hurried to the scene of the crime. Policemen swarmed around the billiard table. The remaining scaffolding listed heavily to starboard, and it looked like a feather would knock it over. Most of it was already down, and under it he could see the dusty tweed of Mr. Boddy's coat.

He studied the scene. There was something amiss. Something he couldn't put a finger on. The tusk still hung suspended through the broken window. The warthog's warts were still sheared off. The gnu lurched at an angle. He could almost see the fleas running in distress across its snout.

No, there was something missing. He would think about it. In the lounge, with his eyes closed, in the green leather chair. Blessed are those who nap, for they shall awake refreshed.

Half an hour later, he sat bolt upright. Of course. The rope. Someone had removed the rope that held the scaffolding together. Why? What was in that room that Mr. Boddy was not supposed to see? A gazelle with moth holes?

No, it was that brittle piece of paper. Mr. Boddy had picked it up after the tusk incident. It had a ragged edge. Perhaps there was more where that came from. Mr. Boddy had gone to find the rest, and someone had made sure he was unsuccessful.

Where had Mr. Boddy taken his paper? To his study.

Mr. Green got up, stretched, and wandered out of the room like a man with no destination. In the front hall, he slipped into the study and closed the door. He only needed to sniff to find the missing paper. Dusty fingerprints were a second clue, leading him to the second desk drawer on the left. He lifted the paper out gingerly and laid it on an open page of his Bible, where he could read it without touching it again.

---

rning my father, I, Hugh Black, do promise
stipend for the rest of his days.
his request in his soldiering career.
th deny responsibility and knowledge of the
ides shot my father.

Interesting. Mr. Boddy needed the other half.

Leaving the study almost as he had found it, Mr. Green watched from the hall until the policemen headed to the kitchen for tea break. He slipped into the billiard room. He had to be quick and quiet. The scaffolding was out of the question. He tested the side table for strength and formed a pile of chairs on it. He positioned his pile under the gnu head and climbed up. He pulled the trophy away from the wall. It came down in a cloud of dust. Trying not to cough, he ran his fingers over the back of the wooden plaque. A brittle piece of paper snapped off some brass tacks and wafted to the floor.

Quickly, he replaced the gnu, rearranged the chairs, brushed off the tabletop, scooped up the paper, and ran from the room. He didn't stop until he was safely in the front hall. He placed the paper on the Louis Quatorze table to examine it. It was brittle, yellowed, and the ink had faded. Nevertheless, he was able to make out the gist of it.

In return for services rendered in Africa conce
to provide Michael Mustard an annual
In addition, I shall endeavor to assist him at
If this matter is ever questioned, we shall bo
event, claiming one of the native gu

He smoothed the paper between the pages of his Bible.

Mr. Green wandered down the passageway, until he found his quarry alone in the library, relaxing in the gray wingback chair with an atlas. He closed the door behind him. "I accuse you of killing Mr. Boddy in the billiard room with the rope," he said.

HEADS UP

SOLUTION:

"I did no such thing, old chap," Colonel Mustard said. "Whatever gave you that idea?"

"Mrs. Peacock had us moving those wretched heads around as part of her re-decorating scheme. The unfortunate incident with the tusk caused this bit of paper to shake loose." He opened his Bible and exposed the first yellowed sheet. "John Boddy picked it up. You suggested it might be the provenance of the gnu. It isn't. It's an agreement between gentlemen."

"I dare say there are many agreements between gentlemen lying about in this house."

"There are, one being Sir Hugh's will. Mr. Boddy is about to take control of the estate, and he wondered why you were receiving an annuity. After he found this shred of paper, he went back later to find the other half. You happened on him standing on the scaffolding sliding the gnu off its mooring. You knew the secret lay behind the gnu. So you pulled away the rope that held the scaffolding, and it collapsed, killing him."

"This is all poppycock."

Mr. Green shook his head. "I slipped into the billiard room while the policemen were on their tea break. I climbed up on a pile of chairs. I took down the gnu and found the rest of the paper, tacked to the rear of the mounting board of the gnu."

He produced the second sheet. "If I put the two together, it appears you and Sir Hugh had an agreement. You would shoot his father, making it look like an accident. I suspect Sir Hugh was anxious to get on with his inheritance. Accidents often happen on safari. You were, and are, a crack shot, whereas he was hopeless with a gun, as displayed so eloquently on the trophy walls. In return, he would pay you an annuity in perpetuity. Well, as long as you lived, even if you outlived him. In addition, he would act on your behalf as needed to assist you in your progress as a career soldier. Hugh paid you for twenty-two years. After he died, the estate paid you."

He aligned the two pieces on the library reading table.

In return for services rendered in Africa concerning my father, I, Hugh Black, do promise to provide Michael Mustard an annual stipend for the rest of his days.

In addition, I shall endeavor to assist him at his request in his soldiering career.

If this matter is ever questioned, we shall both deny responsibility and knowledge of the event, claiming one of the native guides shot my father.

"With this knowledge, John Boddy could send you to prison."

Colonel Mustard clenched his lips for a moment. "What do you intend to do?"

"I have several options. I can take this evidence to the police. I can replace the evidence and wait until the police find it. Or I can, for, say, twenty percent of your allowance, keep quiet about it and happen to drop both parts of the paper in the fire."

Colonel Mustard stroked his moustache. "Twenty percent you say?"

"Yes. Not so much as to make it a hardship for you, but enough to make it worth my while."

The colonel nodded. "Twenty percent then, I give you my word. I believe there is a cheery fire burning in the hearth in the lounge as we speak."

DOG
GONE IT

In the lounge, Professor Plum hunted under the chesterfield cushions for yesterday's paper. Today's paper had the crossword solution, and he was sure he had done quite well. Ah, there, on the table under the windows, all yellowed in the sunshine. He tucked it under his arm.

He settled into the green leather chair and gazed around at the pale silk damask walls. He liked this room, with its comfortable chintz furnishings, green velvet drapes and Oriental rug. The Egyptian archeological artifacts on the mantel were old friends, things he had dug up and shipped to Sir Hugh from his summer expeditions. It felt like home, just the place for calm and inspiration when working the crossword, although home had never been this grandiose.

He opened the yellowed paper and compared it to today's fresh white paper. Yes, he had outshone himself with yesterday's puzzle. A bit of a wrong turn on Six Down, which messed up that quadrant, but overall, an inspired showing. He placed the yellowed paper on the inlaid cherry table beside him and turned to today's puzzle. One across. *Silken canine or sheepskin coat.* Six letters. Hmmm.

The lounge door burst open and a huge pastel long-haired dog bounded in, skittered to an abrupt stop on the Oriental rug, and jabbed a long slender black face into the yellowed newspaper on the table. Before

Professor Plum could raise a hand in defense, the dog had plunged its nose into the paper on his knee, bounded away, stopped on its hind legs at the fireplace, and snatched a pack of playing cards off the mantel.

"What the devil?" he managed. Ought he to fear for his life? Certainly he ought to fear for his crossword.

The dog blinked at him and began munching on the deck of cards. His long feathery tail swished to and fro, brushing a porcelain candy dish to the floor.

Miss Scarlet sauntered through the doorway. "I see you've met Tatters. Isn't he beautiful? All that shimmering silvery-gold hair."

"What is he doing? Where did he come from? Watch out for that tail!"

The dog turned, dropped the remaining playing cards, and threw himself with joy on Miss Scarlet's red ruffles. She was thrown backwards by the impact, and landed on the floor with the dog on her chest, licking her face.

"Tatters, get off me or you'll have me in shreds." Miss Scarlet pushed the dog off and regained her footing. She smoothed her frock and sat on the chintz chesterfield. The dog reclaimed his playing cards, leaped up and sprawled beside her on the chesterfield with his enormous head on her lap. He sighed with contentment, and expelled a copious quantity of intestinal gas from his nether region.

Mrs. Peacock appeared at the door, her aqua skirt fluttering. "What's that dreadful smell? Josephine, are you going to let that dog take up all the seating? He ought to be on the floor. And what's he eating?"

"Eating? It looks like the Ace of Spades."

Professor Plum cleared his throat. The smell was not much worse than the pungent aroma from the camels in Egypt. "Miss Scarlet, why is there a dog in the lounge?"

Miss Scarlet stroked the dog's silky head. "One of my friends asked me to look after Tatters while she went on a theatrical tour. He arrived late last night, while you were on your walk to the village. Tatters is an Afghan hound. A show dog. Afghans are known for their long hair. I have to brush him every day, to keep his hair silky. He loves people, don't you, Tatters?"

Tatters thumped his tail on the chesterfield cushions and gobbled up the King of Diamonds.

Mrs. White appeared in the doorway with a handful of letters. "There's a letter for you, Miss Scarlet. An important one, by the fancy envelope. What's that terrible reek?"

Tatters leaped off the chesterfield, stuck his hairy face in Mrs. White's hands, selected a smooth white envelope, and raced out of the room with it.

Mrs. White shrieked and gave chase.

Miss Scarlet picked up the dropped letters. "Oh, goody. A letter for me."

"Don't you think you ought to go and get your dog under control?" Professor Plum asked.

She shrugged. "He'll be all right. He'll be back in a few minutes. I've got the Nine of Hearts here. He'll remember it, you'll see." She cut open her envelope and read her letter. Smiling, she tucked it in her pocket and sashayed out of the room. "Here, Tatters, come. Nice doggie."

Professor Plum returned his attention to the crossword. One across. *Silken canine or sheepskin coat.* Six letters. Too bad 'Tatters' had seven letters, as he was certainly a silken canine. Although he in no way resembled a sheepskin coat. Maybe 'hound' would fit. No.

It was no use. The tumult echoing down the passageway—the dog barking and Mrs. White shouting—ruined his concentration. He might as well set the crossword aside and follow the commotion. Further along the passageway, Mr. Green was leaving the billiard room and approaching the uproar. They arrived at the library together, and found Mrs. White, Tatters, Mr. Boddy, and Colonel Mustard engaged in a lively tableau.

Colonel Mustard slashed at the air with his riding crop from the safety of the gray wingback chair. Mrs. White wrestled the dog for the purloined envelope. She won. The dog barked his disapproval. John Boddy snatched the envelope from her hands and held it high out of the dog's jumping reach. Professor Plum could see the envelope was addressed to Mr. Boddy.

Mrs. White swatted at the dog with her duster. "Get down, you lumbering great brute."

The dog snatched her duster and ran to the far side of the table, as if challenging her to play a game of chase. Mr. Boddy took his letter to his study, shaking his head.

Colonel Mustard relaxed in the gray wingback chair. "Rum sort of dog, what? No end of trouble. Miss Scarlet wants to exercise a little more command of the situation. Make the bounder mind."

The dog dropped the duster and cuddled up to the colonel. No sooner had the colonel smiled and given it a scratch behind the ear, than it poked its long snout into his pocket and came up with his passport. It sprinted to the corner of the room and pulled out several pages to chew.

Colonel Mustard yelped, sprang up, and swatted at the dog with his riding crop. He missed. The dog dropped the passport and ran for cover behind Mr. Green. Once there, he dug his nose into Mr. Green's jade silk trouser pocket and came up with a mouthful of pound notes.

Mr. Green shrieked. The dog absconded down the hall, Mr. Green in pursuit.

Colonel Mustard collected the shreds of passport papers. "As I said, Miss Scarlet ought to pay more attention. Dog's a public enemy."

Mrs. White retrieved her duster. "No end of trouble, he'll be. Like as not he'll knock me down when I've a full tray of tea." She sighed and left in the direction of the kitchen.

"Miss Scarlet ought to pay more attention." Mr. Green returned, fanning the air with his leather-bound Bible. "I think that dog needs to go out. I hope she figures that out before it's too late. Three pounds, he's cost me this morning. Ate those pound notes like they were a packet of crisps."

Professor Plum thought of what the consequences might be if they all waited for Miss Scarlet to figure something out, when the object in question was a dog of dubious digestive fortitude. He followed the shouting to the kitchen, where Tatters was yanking the duster out of Mrs. White's apron pocket. He opened the back door, and called out, "Tatters? Want to go out?"

The dog abandoned the dust rag and sprinted through the door to freedom.

Mrs. White retrieved her duster. "Thank you, Professor. That was most kind of you. That dog was trying to eat this. What kind of dog eats rags?"

"I wonder if Miss Scarlet has thought to feed it anything respectable."

Mrs. White glanced around the kitchen floor. "I don't see a water dish or food dish within its reach. I'll set something out. I've a little meat in the pantry that's gone green."

Professor Plum wandered into the conservatory and watched through the windows. Tatters was standing hip deep in the ornamental pond, lapping ferociously. He snuffled around the shrubs for some twenty minutes, found some amenable to his purpose, made his contributions to the enrichment of the soil, and returned to the house. He barked once, sharply. When the door failed to open, he hurled himself at it.

This wouldn't do, having the doors battered down by a dog. Professor Plum let Tatters in and went in search of Miss Scarlet, to advise her of the responsibilities of dog ownership, even if the dog was only rented.

In the passageway at the front of the house his progress was halted by Colonel Mustard, puffed up to his finest.

"Can't let you proceed on this route, my boy. Boddy's come a cropper in the study. Please regroup in the lounge." Colonel Mustard tapped his riding crop on the floor for emphasis. "Chop chop. On the double."

Professor Plum hurried to the lounge.

He was the last to arrive. Mrs. Peacock and Miss Scarlet sat side by side on the chintz chesterfield. Mr. Green sat in one green leather chair. Mrs. White perched on a small straight-backed wooden chair. Tatters sat comfortably in the other green leather chair, leaning toward Mr. Green and rolling his eyes. Mr. Green glared at the dog and clasped his leather-bound Bible close to his chest.

"Here's the professor now, and nowhere to sit," Mrs. White said. "Someone ought to shift that dog."

"Here, Tatters, come, good doggie," Miss Scarlet crooned. "I guess he doesn't want to move. Professor Plum can sit on the edge of the table. I'm sure we won't be here long. The colonel will sort everything out."

The door opened. Colonel Mustard stepped in and fastened the door behind him. "Company, at ease. The authorities want us to remain together. They'll be asking us questions presently. I'm sure we can all assist them with their inquiries. They'll want to see this piece of paper I found under the body." He patted his breast pocket. The dog stared at him intently.

"What's happened to Master Boddy?" Mrs. White asked. "Did that dog gnaw his leg off? Miss Scarlet didn't feed it, you know."

"Don't think the dog had anything to do with it, unless he can wield a candlestick," Colonel Mustard said.

"That dog better shift." Mrs. White stood, fist clenched.

"Tatters can sit there if he wants to," Miss Scarlet said. "I'm the lady of the house now."

The only sound in the room was the hissing of air from the dog's rump.

"You what?" Mrs. White dropped back into her seat.

"Yes, you see, I'm John Boddy's sister." Miss Scarlet fluttered her long eyelashes.

"You are, my Aunt Fanny, pardon my French." Mrs. White glared at her. "Just because you've a family resemblance with those dark eyes, don't think you can get away with crazy pronouncements."

"They aren't crazy. I have proof." Miss Scarlet reached in her pocket and pulled out a folded paper. "This is my birth certificate. It says I am the daughter of Margaret Black Boddy and Samuel Boddy, born in Egypt in 1904." She spread it on the closest table for all to see.

"Miss Margaret disappeared in 1904. Her and Mr. Samuel both." Mrs. White frowned. "They were traveling in Egypt. They'd been gone for several months, and then we stopped hearing from them."

"You're Mrs. Peacock's daughter," Colonel Mustard said. "Born after she married James Scarlet, in 1901."

"No, you're wrong," Miss Scarlet said. "I was born in 1904. I'm not a day older than twenty-two. After Margaret, my real mother, disappeared, Mother took me in and raised me." She raised an eyebrow at Mrs. Peacock. To Professor Plum it looked like an actor giving another actor a cue.

"But this paper says otherwise," Colonel Mustard said. "I found it under Boddy's hand. He'd just received it in the post." He pulled a paper out of his pocket. "This is a birth certificate for one Josephine Scarlet, born to Patricia and James Scarlet in, dash, I can't read the date, the dog's eaten that corner."

Tatters lunged off the green leather chair and snatched at the paper in the colonel's hand. The colonel fought to keep it.

In the confusion, Professor Plum slipped into the empty chair. Let the dog take the floor. That's where he belonged.

When order was restored, the colonel was again at his post, the remains of the paper inside his pocket, and the dog eyeing him with suspicion from his new position beside the chesterfield. Another ominous hiss emanated from him.

"Colonel? Do you suppose we could have the door open to circulate the air?" Mrs. Peacock asked. "Tatters is quite pungent."

The colonel nodded and opened the door, but he stood guard so no one could leave.

"Mother? You were about to say something?" Miss Scarlet prompted.

"I was? Oh, yes. Margaret Boddy and I met in 1898, while I was traveling in America. She and Samuel lived in Boston where he was a journalist and author. When I met them again in 1904 in Egypt, they had a brand new baby. There was some civil unrest at the time, and they couldn't get word home. Margaret made me promise if anything happened to her, I'd look after her little girl. And so I did. And here I am." She shrugged.

"That sounds completely plausible to me," Mr. Green said. "As Mr. Boddy has unfortunately passed away, without a wife or heirs, the estate must surely transfer to his nearest living relative, his sister. Blessed are the survivors, for they shall inherit."

"It's all a pack of lies," Mrs. White said, crossing her arms over her apron.

"I think we ought to consider the possibility," Colonel Mustard said.

Professor Plum sensed eyes on him, waiting for him to take a side in the dispute. He picked up the four of clubs from the table and used it as a pointer. "I accuse you of killing John Boddy in the study with the candlestick."

DOG GONE IT

SOLUTION:

"Don't be absurd." Miss Scarlet sniffed and patted the dog.

"No, I'm quite serious. It's the dog, you see, who gave the game away."

"How so?"

"He's been eating things. Playing cards, money, passports, letters. But not the newspaper. I asked myself, what do those things have in common? The answer – they're all made of rag paper. Important documents intended to last are printed on rag paper. The Bible is printed on rag paper, and watercolors are painted on rag paper. I know this newspaper isn't because it goes yellow in the sun. Rag paper doesn't. Tatters has an appetite for rag paper."

"I don't see how this proves anything."

"It does, actually. Most of the things the dog has eaten today are government papers. A passport, money, the birth certificate we found under John's hand. But Tatters is not attracted to the birth certificate proving you are Margaret Boddy's daughter. He didn't select it from Mrs. White's hand when it was delivered. He didn't try to steal it from your pocket. He doesn't care a fig for it now, lying on the table. Because it isn't on rag paper. It's on ordinary paper. The government always uses rag paper for important documents. So your birth certificate is a phony. A forgery."

Miss Scarlet glared at Mr. Green. "You promised me a first-rate certificate. How could you make such a mistake?"

Mr. Green shrugged. "I thought it would be on rag paper. New suppliers. Sorry."

Mrs. Peacock sniffed. "I told you it wouldn't work, Josephine. You never think ideas through. You're too impulsive. If you'd thought to feed the dog, he wouldn't have had to help himself."

Tatters thumped his tail against the chesterfield leg. With one swift move he snatched Mr. Green's leather-bound Bible and raced out of the room.

SWASHBUCKLE

Colonel Mustard spirited a sheaf of blank paper and a couple of pens from John Boddy's desk. Young lad would never miss them. Didn't need to generate income by the pen. Close the study door gently. No one would ever know. They were all in the lounge, awaiting elevenses. He wandered in to join them like a perfectly innocent man.

"Oh, there you are, Colonel," Mrs. Peacock said. "We thought you had gotten lost in the passageways. Mr. Green was about to send out a search party, weren't you?"

Behind her at the curio cabinet, Mr. Green fumbled a porcelain figurine out of his pocket and back onto a shelf. "What, yes? Oh, yes. Blessed are the prodigal, for they shall be gathered into the fold."

"Just taking a constitutional. Never fear." Now here was opportunity. Mr. Green was standing and the second leather armchair was vacant. He nipped in smartly and sat down. There. Comfort.

"I say, does anyone know another word for *bandolero*?" Professor Plum asked, his pen paused over the newspaper crossword puzzle.

"Highwayman?" Mrs. Peacock suggested, rethreading her needle with aqua thread. "Corsair?"

"Torn a hem, have we, Mrs. Peacock? Dashed awkward, high heels." Colonel Mustard smoothed his paper on his knee. Mrs. Peacock must be rather hard up to be doing her own mending. "Buccaneer? Privateer?"

Professor Plum scribbled and erased. "None of those work. Writing a letter home, Colonel?"

"No, writing my memoirs. My publisher was completely taken with Chapter One and insists upon seeing Chapter Two." And refuses to afford any more advance payments until he sees it. "Plum, you've had a bit of experience writing. You've produced papers."

"Why yes, I have. Oxford demands it, you know. The British Museum looks for complete documentation on archeological discoveries. I wonder, desperado? No, too long."

"Try rustler," Mr. Green said, settling onto the chintz chesterfield beside Mrs. Peacock. He bounced back up. "Are these yours? I nearly sat on them." He held out a pair of scissors.

Mrs. Peacock smiled and took them, placing them on the table beside her. "How many letters, Professor?"

Mr. Green sat down again, his forest green check suit trousers pleating neatly over his wing-tip shoes.

"Six. Writing is an enjoyable pastime, Colonel. You can get quite lost in it."

Lost in it, he could hardly get started. Hadn't gotten far enough to get lost. If he could coerce someone to write it for him. "Are you nearly finished that puzzle, Plum? I wonder if you might lend a little of your expertise. I'm trying to write the story of the Siege of Tsumeb but I can't seem to do it justice. If you could see your way clear to writing a bit—I'll dictate, of course—I could see how an expert does it."

"Viking, outlaw, picaro," Mrs. Peacock said.

"I say, Mr. Green has writing experience, too," Professor Plum said, hugging his crossword. "He writes sermons."

Mr. Green flicked a bit of aqua thread from his suit lapel. "I don't so much write them as they write themselves. I just make a note or two. I don't think I can be of much help, Colonel. Where is that Mrs. White with the coffee?"

The door swished open.

"Here's the tray then," Mrs. White said. "Coffee and Hamilton gingerbread."

Miss Scarlet burst through the door hard on Mrs. White's heels, dragging John Boddy by the sleeve. "Is the coffee here?"

"Looter, raider, pirate." Mrs. Peacock held up the hem of the aqua flowered garment lying across her knee.

"Pirate. That's it. Thank you." Professor Plum printed in the squares, chuckling.

"Pirate! See, John, everyone thinks it's a good idea. Don't you, Mother?" Miss Scarlet swooped in on the silver tray so fast her garnet frock twirled around her knees.

Mrs. Peacock snipped her thread and replaced the scissors on the table with a pointed look at Mr. Green. "Whatever are you talking about, Josephine?"

"I've just been telling John how exciting it is in Hollywood. I think he and I ought to take a trip there after his birthday. He could visit his old home, and we could go to the moving picture companies. Douglas Fairbanks and Mary Pickford can't last forever. After all, Douglas is forty-three. How much longer can he go on leaping onto castle walls, swinging from drawbridges and saving the heroine? John is perfectly suited to the job. I could be his leading lady. We'd make millions."

"Millions of enemies?" Mrs. Peacock asked. "Millions of blunders?"

"Money, Mother, money. People go to see moving pictures like *Robin Hood* and *The Thief of Bagdad* over and over. They're most popular. Imagine John as a pirate, sword-fighting his way down the gangplank, swinging from the rigging, rescuing me from death at the hands of the brigands."

"Brigands! Thank you, Miss Scarlet. I think that's twelve down." Professor Plum scribbled in letters.

Colonel Mustard tucked his papers under the seat cushion. He was getting nowhere with his story, and John Boddy was leaning on the mantel sipping coffee. He might notice the paper bore his letterhead. "Fancy a change of scenery, then, Boddy?" he asked. "A tour of America sounds just the ticket. You could visit the old homestead, see the Statue of Liberty, even pay a visit to Mr. Green's alma mater, and tell them what a fine preacher he became."

Mr. Green choked on his gingerbread. "No point it visiting the seminary," he said. "Closed to visitors. They like to keep the minds of the students on a higher plane. Blessed are the focused, for they shall graduate."

Mrs. Peacock raised an eyebrow. "I've never heard of a school closed to visitors. Usually they welcome guests, in case you want to send your children there."

"And the parents don't know well enough to stay away," Miss Scarlet said, with a glower for her mother. "Think of the fun we'd have, John, strolling around Boston, seeing your old house and school. We might even get invited to the Boston Tea Party. I shall need a new hat, of course. I can't go to a tea party in last year's hat."

Mrs. White refilled everyone's cup. "I dare say there'll be many of Margaret Boddy's friends left to tell you what a fine woman she was. I know the banker still remembers her, as he sends a card at Christmas."

Mrs. Peacock frowned at her mending. "John can't just walk into Hollywood and expect to be chosen for a leading role. He needs certain skills. He needs to know how to handle a sword and how to swing from the rigging of a ship. This is a silly notion, Josephine. You ought to forget about it and concentrate on getting a supporting role for yourself in the West End next season."

"Skills! We need to practice. John, I'll get you outfitted as a pirate. I'll bet the Colonel knows how to handle a sword. He'll joust with you." Miss Scarlet waved her hands in a sweeping motion.

"One doesn't joust with a sword," Colonel Mustard said. "One fences with a sword." Zounds, the ideas that ran rampant through this young woman's mind. He hadn't done more than stand at attention with a sword in thirty years of military service.

"There are lots of swords hanging on the walls. Colonel, you get two down and we'll practice in the passageway. Then we need to practice swinging from the rigging. Could the rest of you manage to arrange a pirate set in the ballroom? I'm too busy with costuming." Miss Scarlet grabbed Mr. Boddy's elbow. "Are you finished your coffee? Hurry on. We've work to do. Hollywood waits."

She pushed him out the door before he could protest.

"That sounds like fun, visiting America. I've never been," Professor Plum said. "You've been, haven't you, Mrs. Peacock? Didn't you know Mrs. Boddy?"

"Yes, she and I were friends. John Boddy was only a toddler then. We used to take tea in the afternoons and talk of England."

"Was she happy, do you think, away from familiar surroundings?"

"Happy enough, unless she and Samuel were on the outs. Then she'd threaten to come home."

"Aye," Mrs. White said, "she wrote now and then that she'd sent a friend to buy herself and the boy a ticket on a liner. Next letter, all was patched up."

"You don't really think Miss Scarlet would do it, do you?" Mr. Green asked. "Drag him all across America, visiting houses and seminaries?"

"She'll not let it rest until she meets an obstacle blocking the smooth implementation of her plans." Mrs. Peacock stood up and walked to the window, pushing aside the green velvet drapes. "My daughter is not very good at surmounting obstacles."

Mrs. White gathered the empty cups on the silver tray. "Master Boddy has no call to go traipsing across the ocean. If it's an obstacle that's needed, someone ought to create one." She collected her tray and left the room.

Mr. Green glanced at his watch. "Oh, dear, the time. I must be off." He shot out the door before anyone could ask where he was going.

Colonel Mustard glanced down at the secreted papers. He ought to hide them somewhere else, between the covers of a large book, perhaps. "I'll go and find some suitable swords, then." He took the stolen paper and marched to the library.

First, he found a large book of famous artists, and tucked his purloined paper between the pages. Next, he considered the decorative swords on the wall. Why people thought crossed swords were attractive was anyone's guess. He'd seen enough of swords at work.

This looked like a matched set. Miss Scarlet would want a matched set, for aesthetic reasons. He lifted one off its mounting bracket. No, far too heavy. He couldn't swing it without falling over.

How about this set? No, too sharp. A person could get hurt playing around with these.

What about these? Dull blades, lightweight, tarnished. Just the ticket. But what would he do with them? Hope Boddy hadn't taken fencing classes, for starters. Then again, if he had, the match would be over quickly and Miss Scarlet would proclaim Boddy had passed the test. She'd move on to something else. As long as Boddy didn't leave for America before his imminent thirtieth birthday, he didn't care.

He took a few minutes to practice some thrusts and footwork. He'd seen Douglas Fairbanks at the pictures. How hard could it be?

Quite hard, apparently. Still, he hadn't actually cut his shin.

"Yoo-hoo, Colonel Mustard, where are you?" Miss Scarlet's voice echoed down the passageway. "Here you are, hiding in the library. I told you we were going to practice in the passageway. There's more room to move backward and forward. Come along. Those swords look boring. Let's use those big ones."

"Miss Scarlet, we ought to start small to get the finesse, then move to the bigger ones later, for spectacle."

Miss Scarlet snatched one of the swords from his hand. "I suppose, as you're the expert. Come along."

There was no avoiding it. Unless he could come up with an obstacle he was going to have to fake his way through a sword fight.

In the passageway, Mr. Boddy leaned against the wall staring at the ceiling, like someone who has peeped in the wrong window. His face was the same color as the pink headscarf he wore, which trailed to his elbows. Miss Scarlet had dressed him in large gold hoop earrings and drawn a black moustache on his upper lip. He wore a white shirt open to the waist, high riding boots and buff jodhpurs. The shirt seemed to be chiffon, and billowy about the wrists. If the ancestral portraits surrounding them could see what had become of their progeny, they would curl up in their frames.

Colonel Mustard struggled to keep a straight face. This would be a short sword fight, with two unwilling participants. "Steady on, Boddy, we'll start with the basics. Thrust and parry. We'll do it in a choreographed

fashion, controlled movements. That's the way to learn swordsmanship."
He stepped to Mr. Boddy's side. "Hold the sword thusly. Step forward with
one foot. Thrust. Recover. Other arm out for balance."

Mr. Boddy followed instructions in slow motion.

"Excellent. Now we'll repeat that motion, with both hands on the hilt,
to look more dramatic." Dash it all, these things were heavy when you
started swinging them around.

"This is too boring," Miss Scarlet said. "Too slow and you're both
doing the same thing. Why not jab at each other? I want to see some big
swipes, lunges, pirouettes."

"You'll see blood on that lad's chest if we start lunging at each other."
It made a man wish he was back in the Army, where the ladies went
about their own business and did not obstruct swordsmen. He began a
series of short strokes, and Boddy copied.

"What the devil are you playing at in my passageway?"

Mrs. White's voice unbalanced him, and he swung around in mid-thrust.
A Ming vase took the brunt of it, swept off the table into a thousand shards.

"Now look what you've done! I'll be sweeping for an hour!" Mrs.
White brandished a dust cloth.

"I think John's done very well at swordsmanship, don't you, Colonel?
I think we ought to move on to another skill." Miss Scarlet grabbed Mr.
Boddy's wrist and hauled him away from the scene.

"So sorry. Clumsy of me." He couldn't think of anything else to say.
The Ming was probably worth more than his month's allowance. He
hoped Boddy wouldn't deduct.

Mrs. White seemed cross. Fight or flight. "Excuse me, I must go
and oversee the training in the ballroom." He marched away, swinging
his sword.

The ballroom was chaos. Mr. Green had dragged the grand piano across the floor to a new spot marked with a chalk 'X', and was fussing with the small wheels on the piano's feet. Professor Plum stood on a tall ladder tying a rope to the chandelier. Mrs. Peacock stood on the top of the grand staircase holding the other end of the rope. Miss Scarlet shouted orders that no one listened to. Mr. Boddy stood quietly at the newel post, watching his mansion accosted by a troupe of amateurs.

Professor Plum climbed down off the ladder and moved it to one side.

Miss Scarlet clapped her hands. "Places, people. John, you're going to swashbuckle your way from the top of the staircase to the piano, where the damsel in distress, that's me, waits rescue. This is what Douglas Fairbanks would do: he'd leap from the top of the banister, swing through and grasp the damsel by the waist, then on the backswing drop lightly to his feet and sprint away, carrying the young lady. All right? Understood? Get to the top of the stairs, then. Hurry up, we haven't all day. Mrs. White will be here in a minute to tell us to come for lunch."

John Boddy mounted the stairs like a man climbing to his own execution.

"He ought to have a cutlass between his teeth," Mrs. Peacock said. "Pirates do, you know. Here, John." She handed him a butcher knife. "Here's the rope. Grasp it here and leap off the banister. Your weight will carry you to the piano and back, like a pendulum."

John Boddy climbed onto the edge of the banister as instructed. Mrs. Peacock stepped back against the staircase wall, a hand to her throat. Mr. Green watched from the corner where the piano had once stood, flicking bits of brown powder from his Kelly green sleeves. Professor Plum sat on the bottom rung of the ladder like a spectator at a street carnival.

Colonel Mustard wondered where he ought to stand. Near the door, in case a hasty retreat was in order, although he didn't see any Ming vases in his proximity. He sidled along the hardwood and stopped behind the red velvet divan.

"What's all this topsy-turvy in my ballroom?" Mrs. White's voice echoed off the high ornate plaster ceiling. She stood at the door near the kitchen, mouth hanging open.

No one answered her question. Colonel Mustard wondered how Miss Scarlet would wheedle her way out of this effrontery.

John Boddy eyed the relative distances between banister, chandelier, piano, and floor.

"Oh, come on, John." Miss Scarlet stood with one foot on the piano top and the other on the bench. "If you want to succeed Douglas Fairbanks as King of the Silent Screen, you have to show some gumption."

Mr. Boddy's eyes narrowed. He took the butcher knife from between his teeth and gripped it in his left hand. He jumped, holding the rope with his right hand, his left holding the knife extended as if he intended to impale a fellow pirate with it, instead of rescue a maiden.

The ballroom was silent save for the swoosh as he soared.

Miss Scarlet leaped to the top of the piano in high heels.

The piano tipped. Two legs cracked and buckled. The piano fell to its knees in a symphony of wrong notes. Miss Scarlet followed it down, screaming.

The next King of the Silent Screen kept swinging toward the fair maiden who was no longer in her place.

The rope snapped.

The prospective pirate continued his trajectory while the rope rippled limply behind him.

Mr. Boddy hit the floor somewhere short of the chalked X.

The only sounds were a collective gasp and the clinking of crystals on the wobbling chandelier.

"Oh, I say," Professor Plum spluttered. "Oh, I say."

Colonel Mustard pulled himself together and ran to Mr. Boddy's side. There was no help for him. He turned to the others. "Boddy's come a cropper. Suggest you all leave the room. Professor, go to the study and ring the authorities. Stand clear, chop-chop."

They fled the room en masse. He could hear the echo of feet down the passageway. He'd find them all in the lounge later, no doubt, demanding tea.

Now then, task at hand. Inspect the scene. Lay the blame on others. Not that he had anything to do with this fiasco, but he'd been a party to the sword-fighting portion of the event, and it might reflect badly on him. His record of narrow escapes from culpability was legendary. He was certain he could add another to his score.

He inspected the piano first. Someone had sawed through two of the legs.

He moved the ladder back under the chandelier and climbed to the top. The rope had been tampered with. Many of the inner strands were cut cleanly, while the outer strands had torn from the weight of the neophyte pirate.

He climbed down and removed the ladder. He picked up his sword and ran his fingers along the dull blade. Best confront the villain before alibis had been arranged.

As he suspected, he found them huddled around tea in the lounge.

He marched in and pointed his sword. "I accuse you of killing Boddy in the ballroom with the rope."

SOLUTION:

"Preposterous," Mrs. Peacock said.

"I think not." He swung the sword back to rest, tip on the Oriental rug, and leaned on it with both hands. Dashed thing weighed a ton. "Mrs. White said we needed to create an obstacle to Miss Scarlet's plan of waltzing off to America with Boddy. Many of you agreed with her. Obstacles it is. Neither Plum nor I had a stake in the matter. We did nothing to obstruct Miss Scarlet's plan."

Professor Plum nodded. "I just wanted to work my crossword puzzle."

"Mrs. White didn't want Boddy going away and leaving her here without a salary. Her idea of an obstacle was to interrupt the pirate training as often as she could."

"I was even making shortbread," Mrs. White said. "I knew you'd stop for shortbread."

"Green didn't want Boddy snooping around his seminary."

Mr. Green cleared his throat.

"I suspect there is something at the seminary regarding Green's illustrious career that he doesn't want revealed. Perhaps he didn't graduate and is not an official man of the cloth. Therefore he sawed through two of the legs of the piano, so Miss Scarlet would fall and be injured enough to preclude travel. He has sawdust on the sleeves of his suit."

Mr. Green looked at his sleeves and shook them. A cloud of fine powder puffed around him. "No, there isn't."

"Mrs. Peacock, on the other hand, didn't want Boddy going to see his old home, his mother's friends, or the banker. He'd find Margaret Boddy entrusted sums of money to her friend Patricia Gobelin, to buy her tickets home when she was quarrelling with her husband. Miss Gobelin, now Mrs. Peacock, failed to return those sums of money. She probably used them to purchase her own passage home, first class. If Boddy were to go to visit the banker, he'd find out and demand the money back."

"I'm sure I could have reimbursed him," Mrs. Peacock said.

"I don't think so. I think you are nearly insolvent, or you wouldn't be mending your clothes, you'd be tossing them out and replacing them. You were the person with the scissors, to cut the rope in a way that wouldn't be obvious to the person who climbed the ladder and tied it to the chandelier."

"Well, I never." Mrs. White said.

"There is one other person who tried to create an obstacle. John Boddy removed the knife from his teeth and aimed it to stab the damsel in distress on the piano. He'd rather kill her than go to Hollywood."

"So I managed to save my daughter's life," Mrs. Peacock said. "Pity."

Miss Scarlet stared at her. "Mother!"

"We've only one obstacle left. I smell something burning. I hope it isn't our shortbread."

Mrs. White gasped and fled down the passageway toward the kitchen.

Colonel Mustard sat down on the green leather chair. When the authorities had come and gone, he could resume work on his memoirs again. He could write up the sword fighting scene from the passageway and the near-rescue from the ballroom. The Siege of Tudor Hall, he'd call it. No, that wouldn't do. The Siege of Dhorlltua.

Right. Just the ticket. Now if he could persuade the Professor to do the actual writing. . . .

VOLUME
THREE

Mrs. White stopped chopping liver for the stew. The table had wobbled and spoiled her aim. A pox on that Master Boddy, swiping the book she had under the short leg on the uneven tiled floor. She'd be the rest of the afternoon fighting the liver under these circumstances.

She rinsed her hands and stalked into the passageway to find another. Surely in one of the tables or cupboards which had sat here for four hundred years collecting dust and cobwebs, she could find a loose book nobody would miss.

She ran headlong into Professor Plum, wandering along with his nose buried in the crossword puzzle.

"Oh, my, excuse me, didn't see you coming," he sputtered. "Sorry. So sorry. Clumsy of me." He straightened his purple bow tie.

"No matter. Nothing broken." She smoothed her apron and squared her cap. "Are you finished with that newspaper? It seems about the right thickness, if I fold it up."

Professor Plum hugged the paper to his chest. "Oh, no, I've a few words to guess yet. Can I help you find something else? What are you looking for? Something to fold? Are you doing origami? Making swans from the classifieds?"

"Oregano swans in the classifieds? Is that like fish and chips in newspaper? You do talk in riddles sometimes, Professor." She shook her head. Is that the best they could turn out when they sent young men to expensive schools? "I'm looking for a book to put under the short leg of the kitchen table. I had one, and Master Boddy took it this morning. Just snatched it out, he did, ranting on about value. Got in a right flap about it. It was nothing but an old grey book, Volume Three of something, and just the ticket for keeping the table straight. Anyroad, I'm searching for another so I can get on with the stew." She scanned the closest ebony cabinet. It offered nothing but marble statuettes and porcelain ladies.

"Hmm, I shall help you, then. We can't keep the cook away from the kitchen. About how thick was it?" Professor Plum fumbled his newspaper behind his back, out of her reach.

"About as thick as my finger. And compact, so it didn't stick out and trip me up. A modest book. There must be another suitable one here somewhere. I found that one in a drawer in the ballroom, as I recall, although it was some years ago." She walked across the passageway into the ballroom. The cavernous room resonated with the snoring of an inert figure on the gold brocade lounge seat. She ignored him and went to a large cabinet in the corner. The drawers opened with creaking protests.

"Wha? Who?" Colonel Mustard said, groping for his riding crop and rubbing his eyes. "Must have dozed off for a moment. Pleasant in here, sun in the windows. Forty winks, you know, good for the constitution. What's afoot? Seeking the keys to the kingdom? Scavenger hunt?"

"Scavenger hunt?" Miss Scarlet said from the doorway, in a maroon chiffon frock that vied for attention with the opulent room. "Ooh, that sounds like fun on a dreary day. John Boddy won't talk to me. He's immersed in a private hunt for some rarity in the library. Books, books, books. Where's the fun in that? Shall we hunt for a thimble?"

Mrs. White bit her lip to hold back a rebuke. All she wanted was a book to prop up the kitchen table, and now she had a pack of guests following her around playing at games. The liver would be transmogrified by the time she got back. She'd have to toss in an extra handful of sage to the stew pot to disguise the smell. "Right then," she said. "We're looking for a book about as thick as your finger and as big as your palm."

"That's what John is looking for, and that's too boring," Miss Scarlet said. "I think we should look for something interesting, like a pearl necklace or a pair of shoes."

"Found one," Colonel Mustard said, rummaging in a drawer. "*Treasure Island*. Now there's a book, swashbuckling story."

"Let me see that," Professor Plum said. He took it from Colonel Mustard and flipped it open to the title page. "Oh, my."

"That's my find, so I'll be taking the credit," Colonel Mustard said, trying to retrieve it.

Professor Plum fended him off and took out his magnifying glass.

"Is it total number of items found, or most items found in the shortest time?" Miss Scarlet asked. "Are there extra points for finding books about shoes?"

Mrs. White held out her hand. "I'll take that one, Professor Plum. It looks about right."

"No, you can't possibly use this one to prop up a table leg." Professor Plum clutched it to his chest and his glasses slid down his nose. "It's rare. It's worth hundreds. Thousands."

A curse on that man and his silly ideas. "Right, then, keep on with the hunt," she said with as much civility as she could muster when she had a pile of liver growing moldy in the afternoon sun.

"This is my drawer," Miss Scarlet said to Colonel Mustard. "Go find your own. Oh, look, here's a cuff link. And a silver spoon. I think I ought to get points for finding these."

"We'll never have a winner if we all seek in the same room," Colonel Mustard complained. "I'm going to the library."

Mrs. White sighed. She'd have to find her own book, or dinner would be delayed until tomorrow. Professor Plum was sitting down on the job, burrowed in the book the colonel had found. Miss Scarlet was poking in a drawer too small to hold a book, pulling out hat pins and matches. The colonel had the right idea. The place to find a book was the library.

She left them to it and marched down the passageway toward the library. The colonel hovered in the library doorway, parrying the air with his riding crop.

"Steady on, chaps," he said. "Bit of a sticky wicket here. Boddy's bought it. Chucked it. Snuffed it."

Mrs. White stopped beside him and peered around his elbow.

Master Boddy lay on the copper oval rug surrounded with books. He'd been shot.

Mrs. White gave the colonel a gentle shove out of the way and went to Master Boddy's side. He was a goner, no doubt about it. He wouldn't need the little book any more. She glanced around. Perfect little Volume Three, that fit the table leg to a tee, wasn't there.

"Well, that's odd," she said. "He was all bothered about that book and now he's lost it."

"I say, what's going on?" Professor Plum leaned around Colonel Mustard and gazed at the scene. "Oh dear. Is he dead? I don't feel very well." He rushed across the room to the tall windows and pushed the lace curtains out of the way. One of the windows was propped open, and he breathed deeply of the fresh air.

"Did you find something?" Miss Scarlet asked from the passageway. "I've found a snuff box, it's quite a delight. Is there a prize at the end of the hunt? Is it money?"

Colonel Mustard tapped his riding crop on the hardwood. "Order. I must have order. Clear out, the lot of you. Off to the lounge with you all. Mrs. White will bring a brisk cup of tea. I'll call the authorities."

Miss Scarlet whimpered off down the hall, clutching the little silver snuff box. Mrs. White sighed and moved toward the door. Tea again. And her with liver to chop.

Behind her the library window slammed shut.

"Plum, what are you playing at?" Colonel Mustard bellowed.

"Look, it's *Volume One*, propping the window open. Mrs. White, did you have *Pride and Prejudice, Volume Three*?"

"Yes, that was the name of the book. Useful little thing. But it's missing now."

"This is *Pride and Prejudice, A Novel in Three Volumes, Volume One*. First edition. Printed in 1813. A novel in three volumes. It's worth hundreds. Thousands. Even millions if we have all three volumes together."

Mrs. White frowned. "That's what Master Boddy was going on about. Looking for other volumes. That must be why he's torn all these books down." She started picking up the scattered books. "*Duel at Dawn. Quip and Quote. My Little Horse*. Where's my *Volume Three*, I'd like to know."

"So would I," Professor Plum said. "Let's go to the lounge with the others, shall we? The tea can wait."

Colonel Mustard busied himself at the library window, placing a call on the telephone. Mrs. White accompanied Professor Plum down the passageway. Miss Scarlet followed, but got sidetracked by a small cupboard.

In the lounge, Mrs. Peacock sat curled on the chintz chesterfield, reading a novel. Her periwinkle silk frock sparkled around her as if she were a pool of water in the sunshine. She glanced up. "Oh. I suppose you want to sit down." She considered her feet on the cushions, and the floor where they belonged, but didn't move.

Mr. Green slouched opposite her in a green leather chair, his lime green suit shimmering in the sun, and his thick black book pressed to his chest. His pudgy fingers left damp marks on the leather binding of his book. "Let there be wealth, and there was wealth," he said softly. "The Lord helps those who help themselves to things that will improve their lives. Blessed are the impudent, for they shall not be impeded."

"Don't mind him," Mrs. Peacock said. "He's memorizing prayers. Will there be tea soon, Mrs. White? I'm parched."

"Soon," Mrs. White said. "Have you seen any small books around? About as thick as your finger and as big as your palm. Master Boddy took the one I had. The professor seems to think it's one of a rare trio, and they all ought to be here."

Mrs. Peacock arched an eyebrow. "I think I've seen one or two books around the house. Have you tried the library?"

"Of course I have, but Master Boddy's gone and got himself shot in there, so there's no more looking. Colonel Mustard has chased us all out."

"Oh, my," Mrs. Peacock said. "That's rather unfortunate, isn't it?"

Mr. Green jolted upright. "Shot? Will my services be required for a ceremony? I am a clergyman, you know. Blessed are the wealthy, for they shall receive good service. I shall go and get my rate card." He trotted from the room.

"Professor Plum has a small book," Mrs. Peacock observed. "Will that one do?"

Mrs. White sniffed. "That's his rare edition of *Treasure Island*." The liver would be rare, too, and nobody would eat it. "He doesn't think it's suitable to prop up a table leg."

"I should think not, if it's rare. First edition, is it, Professor?" Mrs. Peacock asked.

"Yes, quite. A marvelous find. Mr. Boddy would be able to sell it for hundreds, thousands, if he were able to sell books, but I suppose not, now that he's dead."

Miss Scarlet bounced in the room, her candy apple red frock all aflutter. "Look what I've found. A quill pen with a silver tip. Is it on the scavenger hunt list?"

"There is no list," Mrs. White said, trying hard not to speak sharply. "Why don't you just see who can find a thin book?"

"Boring, boring." Miss Scarlet waved her quill pen in the air. "I'm going to see how many outrageous things I can find before dinner. Would you like to play, Mother? Professor?"

"Oh, I say, I've no time to play games," Professor Plum said. "I must hunt for Volume Two of *Pride and Prejudice*. If Three was under the table leg and One was propping up the window, then Two must be here somewhere. Together they'd make a brilliant coup. I could write an article about them for the British Museum. Mr. Boddy would make millions. I say, now that he's dead, would the books go to his estate or the person who found them?"

"Mother?"

"I rather think the professor has the better game, finding a rare book. Why don't we try to help him, Josephine? I'm sure the book has a pretty cover. And he'll let you act out the plot this evening."

"Act it out, what a super idea. Right, Professor, where shall we start?"

Mrs. White sighed as they scooted out the door. She would have to keep her toe under the table leg. Back to the kitchen, and finish the stew before they started asking for tea and shortbread. As she feared, the liver had turned color. Well, no matter, a little HP sauce would disguise it.

She had almost finished chopping the vegetables when Miss Scarlet skipped in and started rummaging through the pantry.

"Do you mind not doing that, Miss Scarlet? I have a strict order in there for the foodstuffs."

"I won't be half a jiffy. This is such a good game. Professor Plum is searching the conservatory, Mother is in the billiard room, and Mr. Green is playing, too. He's in the study. I'm afraid Mr. Green might win, though. There are lots of books in the study. He elbowed me out and slammed the door. Oh, look what I've found—revolver in the potato bin."

"Give that here," Mrs. White said. "Can't have the guests running about with guns. Someone might get shot. Now off with you and find me a thin book."

Mrs. White made a pot of tea and placed it on the silver tea tray. She put the revolver beside it. Down the hall, she stopped at the library and served the Colonel, who was standing guard at the door. "Here you are, then, a cuppa and a cake. Here's a revolver, too. Miss Scarlet found it in the potato bin. Like as not it's the one Master Boddy was shot with. I expect the authorities will want to examine it."

She left him turning the revolver over and over in his hands and carried the tea tray to the lounge. Empty. They were all busy with Professor Plum's book hunt. She sat down in a green leather chair and put her feet up. That was better. A hot cup of tea and a little sit-down, nothing like it to sort out a bothersome day. Lumpy seat, though. She slid her hand down beside the cushion.

Her hand came up gripping a thin grey volume labeled *Pride and Prejudice, A Novel in Three Volumes, Volume Two.*

She flipped it open. It had nothing to recommend it. Small print, dusty pages, a slight smell of mold. If the professor didn't give back Volume One, she could use this one under the table leg. And here they were, the lot of them, swooping into the room like vultures for the tea.

"Mrs. White! You've found it! Have you found it? I think you've found it." Professor Plum snatched it from her hands. "There, Volume Two. Now all we need is Volume Three and we've the set. Brilliant! Look everyone, Mrs. White's found it." He turned around and brandished the book in the air. "It's worth hundreds, thousands, millions."

"We don't have Volume One," Mr. Green said, stroking his leather book with moist fingers. "We'll have to keep searching. Blessed are those who seek, for they shall be found out. Why don't you let me hold that for safekeeping, Professor?"

"Can we stop for tea?" Miss Scarlet asked. "This hunting game makes me thirsty."

Mrs. White stood up. Some things are better said standing up. "I accuse you of shooting Master Boddy in the library with a revolver."

VOLUME THREE

SOLUTION:

Mr. Green squeezed his leather book to his chest. "Why would I do such a thing?"

"For the sake of a trio of books. Master Boddy took Volume Three from the kitchen and went searching for One and Two. He must have found Two, and showed you the pair. You shot him and took both. Professor Plum found One in the window, but you didn't know that as you'd left the lounge before the professor told Mrs. Peacock about it. So while the others were hunting for Two and Three, you were seeking One. I've found Two in the chair you were sitting in."

"That doesn't mean anything," Mr. Green said. "You could have put it there yourself."

"Why would I put it under the cushion when I need it under the table leg? I dare say we shall find my little missing Volume Three inside your black book." She pulled it from his hands and let it fall open. A thin book with a dent in the cover slid out. "There it is. Master Boddy had it when he left the kitchen."

Mr. Green sighed. "You have no idea how much that's worth."

"No, but Professor Plum does, and he's got Volume One rolled up in his newspaper, haven't you, Professor?" Mrs. White nodded at the paper tucked under the purple tweed sleeve.

"Well, yes, I do. After I found it in the window I had to protect it." Professor Plum unrolled the paper and exposed Volume One.

"There, that's all looked after then, except for one last detail," Mrs. White said. "Who's going to find me a book to prop up the kitchen table leg?"

THE
GAME'S
AFOOT

The scent of coffee billowed through the lounge door when Colonel Mustard opened it. Nothing like a bracing cup of coffee to tide a man over until lunch. Especially if there was a currant scone or treacle tart to accompany it. The tinned sardine atop a boiled egg had not been the most salubrious of breakfasts. He depended on this morning's baking.

Miss Scarlet was sprawled on the chintz chesterfield, her full coffee cup balanced on her forehead and her rose pink satin dressing gown heaped around her. "Bored, bored, bored. I am so bored," she said.

Colonel Mustard surveyed the others. Mrs. Peacock sat rigid with disdain in one of the green leather chairs. Professor Plum occupied the other, artificially engrossed in the newspaper. Mr. Green stared out the window, fingering the green velvet drapes. Mrs. White rattled the china cream and sugar on the silver serving tray.

Any fool could see no good could come of this.

In two strides Colonel Mustard was across the room. In three strokes he had commandeered a cup of coffee and four butterscotch meringues. Within the minute he had exchanged pleasantries and exited the room.

I'm bored. He had no intention of listening to that twaddle until noon. *I'm bored.* If the lass would shift herself into something constructive, she would not be bored. This mansion was full of interesting nooks and delightful bric-a-brac. The library overflowed with books. The newspapers arrived twice daily. The billiard room offered a game whenever the mood struck. How could she be bored?

He ought to go there now. A lazy round of billiards, perhaps open up the dart board and exercise his throwing arm. Just the ticket.

The billiard room glowed in the morning sunshine, the taupe drapes and walls allowing full focus on the trophies and ribbons displayed on every shelf. Some members of the Black and Boddy families had been great sportsmen. Hunting, fishing, riding, cricket, polo, tennis, shooting. How did a family become such heroes?

Encouraging games and sports in the young. That was it. Get the youngsters playing games from an early age, and by the time they'd grown, they'd developed all kinds of skills.

He'd not much opportunity to excel at games when he was growing up. He'd played school sports, but his father had not put much stock in them. The military family life placed the focus on other pursuits. He'd learned to be a crack shot with a rifle.

He selected a billiard cue from the rack and lined up the balls.

What was this, on the other side of the table, huddled in the corner?

John Boddy. Dead, it looked like. Head crumpled in a fashion that indicated repair was not possible.

Colonel Mustard replaced the cue on the rack and knelt beside the deceased. His right hand rested on a page, dove grey letterhead, a formal declaration waiting to be signed with the black pen that lay nearby. Mustard retrieved the paper.

I, John Boddy, do hereby rescind and revoke the following allowances, formerly paid by Sir Hugh Black of this estate to the following persons:

Colonel Mustard rocked back on his heels. His name was on the list.

As were the names of the other five people in the house. Boddy had asked them here to his thirtieth birthday party, on which day he received the entire estate, and he was going to sever their allowances. Colonel Mustard clutched his heart. How could he manage without Sir Hugh's money? How could Boddy have such callous disregard for the comfort of others?

Boddy'd not see that thirtieth birthday and inheritance now. Someone had killed him to stop him from signing the paper rescinding the allowances. Why not beg, plead, cajole? Stay at the mansion all summer if necessary, talking him around. Killing him seemed a little extreme.

Most unsportsmanlike.

Ah-ha. To expose the culprit, he need only to discover who didn't play fair.

Games, games, games. He'd sort out that bored young woman at the same time.

First he poked into Boddy's pockets and found three pound notes. Good. The prize money.

Where would a family store the games of childhood? He opened the closet near the door of the room. Quite so. A treasure trove. He selected a number of items and carried them down the passageway to the lounge.

Miss Scarlet lay on her stomach on the chesterfield, one hand drawing designs on the Oriental rug, a foot in the air twirling a pink slipper. The mood in the room was much as before, glowering.

"Right, all of you, on your feet," he demanded. "We're going to have a Sports Day. Activities on the lawn. Horseshoes, croquet, tennis, three-legged races, and perhaps that one where you carry an egg on a spoon in your teeth." He displayed his armload of sports gear.

"I think I shall pass on this," Mrs. Peacock said, picking up a book from the table beside her chair.

"Boring, boring, boring," Miss Scarlet said.

"There are no passes. There is no boring. We have two teams, the ladies versus the gentlemen. Points will be awarded. Cash prizes will be presented at the end of the day."

At the mention of cash, Miss Scarlet's finger stopped moving on the carpet in the middle of a large B.

"I shall expect to see all four of you on the front steps in fifteen minutes, dressed in appropriate sporting attire. That is all." He turned with a snap and marched out, through the front hall and down the steps. He laid the sports gear on the ground in ordered lines, and commenced installation.

It took ten minutes to find the family horseshoe pit, overgrown with ivy. It took another twenty minutes to plot out a course on the lawn for the croquet game and press the hoops into the grass. In seven more minutes he had a string strung between two trees to serve as a finish line for the races, and another laid on the grass to indicate the start line.

The four contestants straggled out to the front steps forty-seven minutes after his orders had been issued. Miss Scarlet looked absolutely fetching in a snowy white tennis dress with coral trim and matching tennis shoes. Mr. Green looked fully prepared in emerald green plus-fours. Mrs. Peacock had changed into a periwinkle pleated skirt and sailor blouse, and had removed her pearl necklaces. Professor Plum remained in his tweed jacket and bow tie. He shrugged, as if indicating he had no other options in his wardrobe.

Mrs. White followed them out with a tray of glasses and a pitcher of water. "Games," she said. "They always make people thirsty."

"How much money do we win if we win?" Miss Scarlet asked.

"This much." Colonel Mustard flashed the three pound notes he'd taken from Boddy's pocket, folded in half so they appeared to be six. He tucked them back into his pocket before they received close scrutiny.

"Is that enough to buy shoes?"

Colonel Mustard lifted the referee's whistle hanging on a string around his neck, and blew it sharply. "First, we'll have a game of horseshoes. Follow me to the pit. I assume you've all played before and understand the rules?"

Professor Plum shook his head. "Not a game to play in Egypt, where I grew up. Too much sand, you see. Too few horses. "

"A review is in order, then. The object of the game is to get your horseshoe as close to the stake in the center of the pit as possible. Three points are awarded for a ringer, getting your shoe around the stake. In the case of no ringers, one point is awarded to the shoe closest to the stake. I shall award additional points for finesse and sportsmanship. Twenty-one points wins the game."

The group gathered at the horseshoe pit.

"Ew, these horseshoes are dusty. And heavy." Mrs. Scarlet held one at arm's length.

"Someone ought to rake the pitching boxes first," Mrs. Peacock said. "It's hardly sporting to contend with ivy tendrils and errant weeds around one's ankles. Mrs. White? Do you have a rake?"

Mrs. White grumbled away and reappeared with the rake, muttering to herself loudly so everyone heard. "The things I have to do. As if I'm not busy enough preparing lunch, and me with the coffee cups to wash and all. I'll be glad to see the back of Master Boddy's birthday party." She gave the sand a cursory raking, yanked out a few ivy plants, and returned to the house.

Colonel Mustard held out the four horseshoes. "Two shoes each. Two teams. Ladies versus gents. Ladies first." He handed two shoes to Mrs. Peacock and two to Mr. Green.

"You said Ladies," Miss Scarlet said. "Mr. Green's on the other team."

"Quite so. One member of your team against one member of the other team."

"This is monumentally dull."

Colonel Mustard blew his whistle. "Deduct one point from the ladies—complaining."

"What's the matter," Mr. Green asked. "Miss Bored can't wait to have a turn?"

Colonel Mustard blew the whistle again. "Deduct one point from the gents—sniping."

Mrs. Peacock sighed. "Oh, for heaven's sake." She threw her first shoe. It glanced off the stake and landed in the sand.

"Lucky toss. Couldn't do that again," Mr. Green muttered. He threw his. It zoomed through the pitch to the grass on the other side.

"A little heavy handed, just like your sermons," Mrs. Peacock said. She threw her second shoe. It landed in the pit.

Mr. Green threw again, wide of the pitch altogether.

Colonel Mustard blew his whistle. "One point to the ladies." He scribbled on a small notepad.

"Mother threw two in the sand. She should get two points."

"That's not how the game is scored. Next players, Miss Scarlet and Professor Plum." Colonel Mustard handed out the horseshoes.

"Me first," Miss Scarlet said, elbowing Professor Plum out of the way. She threw, and her shoe dropped in the grass well shy of the pitch.

"Nice arm," Professor Plum said. "Maybe you ought to throw more than tantrums." He tossed his shoe, and it landed inches ahead of hers.

"You're not so great yourself," Miss Scarlet's second shoe landed wide of the pitch in the bushes.

Professor Plum tossed. His second shoe landed a foot closer to the pitch, but still on the grass.

Colonel Mustard blew his whistle. "One point for Plum. Tie game, one point each team." On the notepad he wrote the score, then added *Deduct one point Miss Scarlet—elbowing. Deduct one point Plum—insults.*

"Can we move on to something else?" Mrs. Peacock asked, wiping her hands on her hanky. "This is tedious."

"Blessed are the tedious, for they shall inherit tedium." Mr. Green said.

Colonel Mustard sighed. "Change ends, throw to the other pitch."

The second end was not much improved from the first. By the time the shoes had been rescued from the shrubs and the ornamental pond, the score was two-all, if he didn't count the deductions. They'd be all day getting to twenty-one. He could not stomach much more bickering.

"Game called," he said, blowing his whistle. "Moving on." He consulted his list. "Perhaps something with fewer rules for the next game. I'll go to the kitchen for eggs and spoons. You may stand down."

He hurried to the kitchen, where Mrs. White stood at the sink, washing coffee cups and candlesticks. "Might I have four eggs and four spoons?"

"You'll find them over there." She pointed with soapy fingers. "Mind you don't let that Mr. Green steal the spoons."

"I'll watch for that. We'll need more water, as well, when we're finished the race."

He left to her annoyed mumblings.

At the start line of the race, he handed out the kit. "This is a simple race. Place the egg on the bowl of the spoon. Place the handle of the spoon between your teeth. Run to the finish line. First one there with egg intact wins. Ready, Steady, Go!"

The four contestants began running. Almost immediately, Professor Plum dropped his egg. He managed to ram into Mr. Green before he dropped his spoon. Mr. Green lost his egg in the collision.

Miss Scarlet was making great strides until Mrs. Peacock trundled up beside her and said, through clenched teeth, "Oh, look, there's the Prince of Wales." Miss Scarlet snapped her head around so fast her egg went flying. It smacked Mrs. Peacock in the ear. The jolt sent her egg flying across the finish line alone.

"There, I win," she shouted.

Colonel Mustard blew his whistle. "I'm afraid you're disqualified. Your egg arrived without you, and is no longer intact. No points."

"Ha," Miss Scarlet said, two hands on her hips. "Serves you right."

"In fact, I am going to deduct one point from Plum for elbowing and one from Mrs. Peacock for unsportsmanlike utterances." On his notepad he recorded they'd been sabotaging their own teams.

"Can we move on to something with less running?" Professor Plum asked. "I think I need a drink of water."

"We'll try croquet. Anyone played this before?"

Mr. Green shook his head. Miss Scarlet shrugged. The others nodded.

"Good. We'll have some semblance of order. To review the rules, the object is to bat your ball around the course under the hoops in the correct order, and back again. Then you hit the center peg with the ball, and it is taken out of play. The winner is the team to have both balls out first. When it's your turn, if your ball goes through a hoop or hits another ball, you play again. You play until you miss doing either." He lined up the balls on the grass. "Red, yellow, black, blue."

"I'll take blue. I always take blue." Mrs. Peacock picked up the blue ball.

"I absolutely must be red," Miss Scarlet said.

"I suppose I can be black. No, yellow. No, black." Professor Plum scratched his head.

Mr. Green grabbed the yellow ball. "What's to decide? They're just colors."

"No, they're teams," Professor Plum said. "Black and blue are a team. Red and yellow are the other team." He glanced at the two ladies. "I suppose I'm black, playing with Mrs. Peacock."

Mr. Green looked at his yellow ball, and the red ball in Miss Scarlet's hands, and sagged.

"Let's begin. The play is blue, red, black, yellow, in that order. Start on the baulk line."

Mrs. Peacock strode up to the line, placed her ball, and whacked it firmly with her mallet so it rolled under the first hoop and halfway to the second.

She moved forward and hit again, but her ball sliced to one side.

"Red," Colonel Mustard called.

Miss Scarlet hit her ball with such ferocity it bounced over the first hoop and rolled out of court.

"Move that to the yard line, Miss Scarlet. Black!"

Professor Plum sliced his black toward the first hoop, but it rolled short.

Mr. Green stepped up and swung his mallet like a golf club, sending his yellow ball into the horseshoe pit.

"Wrong stance, Green," Colonel Mustard said. "Swing as Mrs. Peacock demonstrates. I'll allow you that as a free swing and you can try again."

"Favoritism," Mrs. Peacock protested. "Move on to blue." She took a swipe at her ball and sent it through the second hoop.

Before she could hit again, Miss Scarlet smashed her ball into the court and it ricocheted off a hoop, hitting the blue ball and forcing it into a bad position.

"I beg your pardon, Josephine, it was still my turn."

"Too bad. It's not your turn now."

"I'm going next."

"No, you're not."

"Mr. Green, get your mallet out of my way."

"Professor Plum, blessed are the players who keep out of my way."

"I say, you stepped on my ball."

"You hit that ball twice."

"Did not."

Colonel Mustard shook his head as he wrote down infractions of the sportsmanlike conduct rules. It was a free-for-all. Mallets were swung too high, nearly clocking heads. Hoops were scored in the wrong order. Balls of all colors moved in unison instead of in succession, clapping into each other and changing the face of the game on the fly.

There was only one saving grace to the whole exercise. He stepped onto the court, watching out for his shins. "Miss Scarlet, are you bored?"

Miss Scarlet paused in mid-swing. "Why, no, I'm not. I am having fun. I'd have even more fun if Mother wasn't such a hog with the mallet. It's my turn, you know. You cheated on that last swing."

"I did not. You said you knew how to play. You've defrauded your partner out of more strikes than I've got pearls."

Colonel Mustard sprang back out of the line of fire. He found Mrs. White standing on the sidelines, watching.

"Cheery game, isn't it?" he asked.

"There's none of them good at games." She shook her head. "Can't play by the rules, any of them. Always thinking of themselves. I'll have to peel extra spuds for dinner. They'll be hungry after this outing."

"Score! I win!" Mrs. Peacock shouted. "Take that, you incompetent clods."

Colonel Mustard thought by the looks on the faces of the others, he ought to blow the whistle. "Game over. I suggest we collect in the lounge for the presentation of the award money. Mrs. White, would you bring tea?"

"Tea, spuds, dinner. It's all the same." She trudged back to the house.

Colonel Mustard made a note about Mrs. White's unsportsmanlike conduct as a game supporter.

As the players vanished into Tudor Hall, he collected the sports equipment and returned it to the billiard room closet. He paused at the trophy cabinet. There was nothing better to end a Sports Day than a trophy presentation. This one at the back ought to do. *Contributions to School Sports Day. John Boddy. Obsidian College.* When he reached the lounge, they were draped on the chairs like marathon runners after a race. Mrs. White poured tea from the silver teapot.

Colonel Mustard held up the trophy in one hand and the wad of prize money in the other. "Excellent games today. We ought to do it again sometime. Before I present the awards, I must make an announcement. Boddy has been murdered." He pointed with the trophy. "I accuse you of killing Boddy in the billiard room with the candlestick."

THE GAME'S AFOOT

SOLUTION:

"What do you say? Mr. Boddy is dead?" Mr. Green leaned forward in his chair.

"Afraid so. Nothing to be done, of course. Gone after breakfast. I've called the authorities and they'll be here soon."

"After breakfast?" Mrs. Peacock asked. "You mean to say all this time we've been outdoors playing silly games, he's been lying there dead? That is outrageous."

"Quite. I used the Sports Day to reveal the killer. I was looking for someone unsportsmanlike. Someone who would rather kill Boddy than risk losing his or her allowance from the estate."

"We're going to lose our allowances?" Professor Plum asked, his bow tie bobbing. "Oh, I say. Whatever shall I do with no job and no allowance?"

"You? You can get a job, that's what you can do. What can I do?" Miss Scarlet wailed. "All this season's plays are cast. Mother?"

"Don't look at me, Josephine. I've nothing to spare. Go and get a job in an office or something."

Mr. Green looked at his hands. "Losing my allowance? Excuse me, I must make some calls." He rose and headed for the door.

Colonel Mustard blocked him with the trophy. "Sit down, old chap. I have discovered the culprit."

Mr. Green returned to his seat on the chintz chesterfield, looking with suspicion at Miss Scarlet beside him. She drew away from him.

The Colonel dropped the trophy on a nearby table and folded his arms across his chest, but carefully so as not to hide his medals. "As I was saying, you all failed the sportsmanlike conduct test. Even Mrs. White, who was unwilling to provide materiel support. So I asked myself, what would I do if Boddy cut my allowance on his birthday? I would stay here for as long as I could, pleading my case. After all, it's a roof, a warm bed and three square meals a day. I conjectured the rest of you would do the same. What would be the net result? Five extra people in the house all summer."

By the way everyone was looking at his or her toes, fingers, or nearby floor, he deduced he had correctly assessed the situation. "Thus the person who had the most to lose was Mrs. White, who would lose her allowance and have to carry on providing for five guests for her regular wages. Plus I found her in the kitchen washing the candlesticks. One doesn't wash candlesticks, one polishes them. She was washing off the evidence of contact between the base of that candlestick and the top of Boddy's skull."

Mrs. White crossed her arms over her apron. "He's right, you know. Master Boddy had a pen in his hand, ready to sign the statement. You'd have all stayed on for months, working your way back into his favor, and Master Boddy wouldn't have tossed you out. I couldn't bear the thought. This way we all keep our allowances."

"Hmm, I rather like the thought of that," Miss Scarlet said.

"As do I," Mrs. Peacock said. "Is there any more tea in that pot?"

Colonel Mustard allowed himself a slight private smile. He'd played a good game, entertaining the troops while unmasking a criminal. He pocketed the prize money and reached for a teacup.